NU-PIKE PRESS

JACK GRISHAM

THE
PULSE OF THE WORLD

NU-PIKE PRESS/PUNK HOSTAGE PRESS

THE PULSE OF THE WORLD
Copyright 2021 by Jack Grisham

For information address:
Nu-Pike Press
P.O. Box 735
Huntington Beach, California 92648
nupikepress@gmail.com

Editor
Melissa Elhardt
Cover Art
D.W. Frydendall

To
ELENA CHANCE

THE
PULSE
OF
THE
WORLD

CHAPTER ONE—THE STRUT

Sometimes you gotta bust a few heads to check the pulse of the world.

I threw a vicious elbow that split the manscaped brow of a valley boy poseur.

Man, it sure felt good to hear that crunch.

I smiled as the boy went down.

"It's all fun and games until you lose an eye—ay, fucker?"

Ha! Little prick—shouldn't be dancing in a man's world. Oh well—punks these days—fucking pussies. When are they gonna learn that there's nothing like a little sock-em-up to make the night turn right—biscuits, gravy, and a big ol' fucking black eye—that's the way we do it.

I checked my groove. The edge of my blade was hard. The strut was on. The pit was tight.

"Hey, what's your problem, asshole?"—the kid from the valley was fronting heavy.

Well, well, well, look who's got sand.

I smiled and kicked the boy in the balls with my black, size-12, motor-cop boots. He dropped like used oil on pavement.

"You better cool those jewels, cupcake."

I was Fred Astaire on a sixer of Mickey's and a whiffed can of aerosol cooking spray. I was beautiful.

My therapist once told me that I was too old for this shit— too old, can you imagine that? That bitch had some fucking nerve. You know what I told her—besides the fact that I fucking love it, I told her that sometimes wild hearts refuse to age—it ain't my fault, it's just the way the cards fall...and 38, well...it's not as old as it used to be—and what do you wanna do about it?

Two of the club's security goons jumped into the pit— *fucking ten-dollar-an-hour hard-ons that don't savvy the spiritual significance of good hardcore and a skin-tight physical groove.*

One of the lurks stepped in my way.

"Hey, Arthur, you were told last week—no more of your bullshit."

"Bullshit? I'm just dancing, man. Check me out."

I did a quick soft shoe in my hard soles, slicked back my hair with an imaginary comb, and then I slapped my wrist as I flashed my middle finger in the goon's face.

"That's for you, fucker."

The beastly cunt took a wild grab. I sidestepped and resumed my roll—singing as I grooved.

"Pushed into a locker and the blood really started to flow...on my shirt...and it hurts, and it's worse now, hey...fuck you, tough guy."

I pulled out my knife and popped the trigger—"Click-click, little boy. I'm coming for you."

The band pumped and spewed as I monkey-danced my way 'round—'picking up change'—and hard swinging to the beat.

I crossed the floor.

The valley boy poseur was up to dance.

Monster, monster, who sees a monster.

The kid threw a crisscross baby-boy punch that on a prayer connected with my right ear. My earring dug a cool translucent orb into my skull.

"Motherfucker—my grandmother gave me those pearls."

I bent down as if hurt, twisted, and came up with a backhand slash that drug the blade across the boy's cheek.

"Gotcha!"

Panic lit the kid's eyes as the blood rocked and bopped thick, warm, and heavy. I cut him again—a quick shallow jab that sharp tickled the boy's rib.

It's all in the style, Baby—we flourish the blade—punk renaissance brushstrokes dancing across a pimpled flesh canvas— slash—slash—slash.

Cold Tijuana steel pogo'd under the stars.

I quick checked the boy's friends.

Little pricks might have been hard before the blood started flowing, but not now—these playschool punkers got no stomach for the real thing.

A foul breath blew bad news over my shoulder—security goon. I rounded and took a cornered-angry-cat swipe.

"Step up, bitch. Come get some, motherfuckers"—I mouthed the words as the booze did the talking.

"We called the cops, Arthur."

The cops?

The band held mid note—the eyes of the audience crawled, full intrigue, up my bladed arm. I laughed and turned to the crowd— "Mommy! That man's got a knife!"

The audience cheered as I held my blade against my throat— "Let 'em come, fuckers. I'll slit my gullet and fuck your beer sales."

I drew blood with the tip.

Greased up, black leathered down—*mine, mine, mine!*

"Arthur! What the fuck, man?" T. Terry's voice fell heavy from the balcony— "Are you fucking kidding me?"

Well, what do we got here, the fucking proprietor, Mr.

T.Terry himself—throwing a limp blanket over my time to shine.

I lowered my knife hand and wiped the blood from my throat.

He wasn't a bad cat—he'd thrown me a job or two—used this shithole as a way to pull ass or whatever else he could turn—threw in the occasional free drink when I was being a good boy. Terry wasn't cool, but he wasn't uncool either—I guess you could say friend, but that's a long shot—more of an easy touch in a closed-fisted world. I don't favor friends.

"Come on, dude!"—Terry pleaded as he descended the stairs—"Walk it off, Chance."

Yeah, Arthur Chance, that's me—walking it off.

The booze took a momentary backseat to reason. I retracted the blade and stepped clear of the goons.

"My apologies, boys."

I pulled up my collar and strolled past the bleeding poseur. I winked wicked at the bruised little man.

"No offense, kid, just getting my thing on."

Fuck, a couple of stitches and a splash of alcohol—he'll be all right. Little fucker should've thanked me—chicks dig scars.

I walked out the door and entered the night.

T. Terry's club, The Crow's Nest, was a few long blocks from my place on the waterfront; and thankfully, the cool night air—instead of sobering me up, it cast a mellow groove atop my buzz.

I don't mind the harbor in the daytime—the seabirds fighting over scraps of what used to be. The constant comings and goings of ships from who knows where to who gives a fuck why. I dig their blind industrial hustle and the sense of superiority I feel when I realize that they think this is what's important, the grab, grab, grab of more, and I know they'll never be satisfied. They'll never know what it feels like to have enough. Yeah, I dig the day—I adore their nonsense, but I prefer the evening—when the stevedores and the big, big bosses have staggered off into the sunset. These are the gentle-

man's hours—the dark hours, when that sweet forgiving mist crawls ashore like a Nubian angel from the ocean, and the foghorns play untethered jazz into the night.

I stopped to piss on the street—fumbled with my buttons, but then urgency forced me to slide my pants off my hips and let loose the stream. I was deep in the flow when car lights lit the street. I stumbled towards the sidewalk as I hiked up my pants and unsuccessfully tried to cut short the stream.

The car advanced.

I reached into my pocket for the blade—it was warm and now piss wet. I leaned into a recessed doorway and waited for the vehicle to arrive.

The faded paint and sea damp wood caressed my back.

The dark machine slowly made its way down the street—intent, looking for something or…someone.

I allowed the shadows of the doorway to remove me from sight.

The car was an expensive black-on-black sedan—too high-end for a late-night trip through the harbor—unless, of course, it was occupied by a couple of spoiled brats looking to get their nasty on. I'll go 10 to 1 that it's that young punk and his getting-braver-with-time friends—little bitches. If they want some, they're gonna get some.

The sedan pulled close enough to touch—heavy, eight-cylinder breath filled the air. A dim interior light revealed a couple—not the boy—a man *and* a woman, in heated discussion. He was letting her have it—*If it got nasty, I was down to intervene; but a Good Samaritan with piss in his pants on a castaway's street isn't an always welcome savior.*

Maybe they were lost. I stayed tight.

The silhouette of the man seemed vaguely familiar—his movements and his manner much like my own. It was too dark to place him.

The car's windows were up; the conversation—hot muted chatter behind smoke tinted glass until…the man's voice shattered the silence.

"He looks like this, you fucking bitch!"

His words were punctuated by a hard, neck-cranking slap to the woman's face. Her head bounced off the window glass, and with eyes rimmed with tears and failing waterproof mascara, she stared like bruised starlight in my direction. I stepped from the shadows. Shock lit her face. She reached for me as the car accelerated and tore reckless down the street. The taillights disappeared into the mist.

This fucking world, man—it's enough to make you put down your drink.

I squared up my piss-*pants* and moved on.

I wound my way through the abandoned field on Central—stepping over bottles and trash—slogging through a rusted metal graveyard of cast-offs that weren't worth a trip to the dump, and then I stood, wavering, one eye cocked, before the old tenement at 215 Broadway—my office home.

The landlord had told me that it was once a brothel, but I didn't give a shit about the old man's fuck-house story. When I signed the papers, I did so because the stairway didn't smell like piss, and from my window, a nice view of the Angel's Gate—the north entrance to the harbor.

I climbed the stairs and paused at my front door. The wood and frosted glass extolled the letters of my trade:

ARTHUR CHANCE
PRIVATE INVESTIGATOR
BY APPOINTMENT ONLY

"Ha!…by appointment only—motherfucker—you got that right."

You know when they say that you were destined for it—that fate dictates career? Well, I don't know much about career, or fate for that matter, but I know my childhood, and I've always wondered what became of my mother, and how anyone, in their right fucking mind, could ever marry that alcoholic cocksucker that I called, Sir.

I hung my leather jacket on a wooden peg. Frank was in the kitchen. It sounded like a plastic bowl was being kicked across the floor—some late-night game that he was playing.

I guess if you gotta have a partner, you could do worse than one who waited up at night for your return. It's just too bad the little fucker can't drive.

I walked into the kitchen. Frank stared at my wet pants.

Fucking cats, man, cold-ass motherfuckers—looking down at the hand that feeds them—as if they're any better.

He jumped onto the table and pushed his head against my hand. I instantly forgave him.

"Yeah, I know, buddy—you're hungry, and I'm a loser—ain't nothing fair in this world."

I opened the cupboard and pulled out a can of Frank's favorite—tuna with liver.

One night—after a few too many, I sampled his meal before I'd blacked-out. When I came to, I was on the floor with an empty tin in my hand and a pissed off cat on my back. I was hoping I dropped before I'd finished the meal, but the way Frank was crying and the foul taste of canned liver in my mouth, I figured the furry little prick went hungry.

I spooned the feline pate' into a bowl and then placed it before the dark grey shorthair. His orange eyes reflected the beginning-to-feel-sober pain on my face.

"There's gotta be a fucking bottle around here."

I searched the kitchen cupboards, the refrigerator, and the pantry. I was considerate of Frank's meal, but…as I continued to come up empty, I became slightly unhinged. I stumbled into the living room and dumped the couch cushions on the floor. I rifled the desk drawers and tore books from the shelves.

I knew I'd be pissed in the morning. I keep a tight house— but when the jones is on, and the liquor store more than a mile away, you aren't exactly tripping on anything but the moment—now, that's the key word—I want it right fucking now.

I paused to think—an uncharacteristic moment of calm settled in my head.

"I know I've got something here. I remember buying it."

A bottle rolled across the linoleum floor. I fled to the kitchen. Frank was playing with a half-filled liter of vodka—Popov, $8.29 a fifth. I kicked at the puss.

"You little fucker. Is this how you treat me? After all I do for you? God damn it, Frank. You are so fucking inconsiderate."

I picked up the bottle, removed the cap, and I tossed it. I took a strong end-of-another-day pull—*instantly satisfied.*

"Fuckin-a man—those vodka connoisseurs talking about, this one is better than that; well, they don't know shit. The best vodka there is—and this is a proven fact, Mr. Frank, is the one in your hand."

I took another drink and winked at my little man—"You want a spritzer?"—no reply.

I walked into the living room and sat on the sofa. The cushions were lying cast-off, like soft pile derelicts scattered about the floor. I let them stay—no sense waking the dead. I returned my attention to the vodka.

It was a rare thing—this unfinished bottle being available— especially with the cap on. You see, I got this theory; you don't need the cap once the bottle has been opened. The cap is for transportation purposes only.

I drained the booze and closed my eyes.

CHAPTER TWO—SOCIETY GIRL

Dreams can be violent, unrelenting companions—especially when the booze—without regard to a peaceful sleep, leaves the gates of awakening open, and the memories of a once forgotten night rush like crazed alleyway thugs into your life.

My father walked into the house and missed the mark as he set his keys upon the counter. They dropped, unnoticed, to the floor. I knew that if he turned left, he'd walk down the hallway, and usually without fit or fanfare, straight to bed—and many an evening that was his road, but tonight he turned right, and the headlights of his drunken rage cast cut razor beams upon my eight year old self.

"Where's your mother, you little piece of shit?"

My trembling hand points toward the bedroom as I shield my shadowed companion from his impending fury.

"Oh, what you got there? A table for two, you crazy fuck?"

He unbuckled his belt.

"You think you can just sit there—doing whatever the fuck you want—watching your fucking cartoons while I work? You think you're a big man?"—He poked at me with his boot—"You're nobody. You're fucking worthless."

I put down my Roll Boy Racer and got to my feet. The walls of our living room contracted as I rose—the lath and plaster conspired to contain me.

"That's right. You stand up when I'm talking to you, so you can see I'm bigger."

My father wiped his slobbering mouth with the back of a dirty hand—"How's it feel to be a pussy?"

The sick un-swallowed scent of bottom-shelf whiskey and beer-back chasers enveloped me as I stepped forward. He smiled— "So you're the tough one, huh? Let's see about that."

"James! Leave him alone!"

My father turned—belt in hand. Cold leather and silver snake buckled anger, once poised to strike a young boy's back, had now set its teeth upon a new victim—my mother.

I heard, but couldn't see as the first blow fell—my father's hulking frame shadowed my view. The second and third strikes raged in violent succession. She dropped to her knees. My father kicked her body against the wall. Unmoving she lay, exposed to his fury. He raised his arm to strike again—the leather belt held limp aloft, but before his downward force could harden its skin, I dug my teeth into his arm—a sting just sharp enough to buy my mother a moment, and to purchase me a rude backhand blow to the face. The floor met my head as I fell.

Lying on my back, blood streaming from my mouth, I stared at him—cold and hard—disconnected from the pain.

"What now, worm, is that all you got?"

He pressed his boot against my chest. His heel begged for a scream that wouldn't come. I refused to cry.

Unnoticed by my father, my mother rose to her feet—in her hand a brass table lamp. She swung the weapon with chipped nail precision. It crashed undefended upon the drunkard's back. He reeled, staggered, retched, but did not go down. She grabbed for my shadowed companion—pulled the figure behind her and called to me, but I was pinned behind my dazed abuser with no hope of escape.

"Give him to me!" she pleaded. "Give me Arthur!"

My father pulled a snub-nose Colt.38 from his shoulder holster—a weapon he used to intimidate street thieves and gutter punks—protection, he called it.

"Not this one, bitch—you keep what you got. I'm leaving."

She reached for me.

My father reached for his keys.

A siren reached for hope in the distance.

I was pulled to my feet and the gun was placed against my head. His finger drunkenly danced against the trigger—"You want me to kill him, Helen?" He backed me into the kitchen—"You think I'm fucking around? Try me."

He'd been known to deliver lie after lie, but this time she swallowed his words.

My mother held her place.

He opened the back door and dragged me downstairs to the parking lot. I was tossed into the back seat of his Mercury and before the police arrived, we were gone.

I opened my eyes. I was still dressed in last night's garb—my boots still on and tied; my mouth tasted like soiled litter box gravel. The cushionless couch had done nothing for my once strong back. I put my feet on the floor and held my head in my hands. The room—slowly spinning, looked as if it had been turned upside down—its contents dumped upon the floor.

"Frank!"

The sound of my own voice, at volume, was at best, abusive. I employed a quieter tone. "You can't stop me before I pull this shit? Come on, man."

The cat was busy elsewhere.

I stripped down and walked into the bathroom. It was occupied. I backed out and half-closed the door—"How about a heads up, Frankie? I'm fucking hurting, man."

I pissed in the kitchen sink. The room slowly stilled.

I don't know how much of that dream was true—if any. My father was a violent, alcoholic, gambler that'd shuffled us from place to place—always off radar. My mother could've been brunette, blonde, or red, and as for Helen...maybe. One night during a drunken rant, my old man had wrestled a specter of that name, but in the morning, there had been, as usual, no discussion. "Sir," as the violent old prick preferred to be called, was short with information and not much for photos—"sentimental bullshit," that's what he called it. Thankfully, when I was twelve, a bullet from the Colt had shut his mouth for good—suicide, they said—a fitting end to that motherfucker. At thirteen, I moved in with my grandmother— although it took the state over a year to find her—and only after I'd been treated to a long and very violent foster home stay with a couple that cared nothing for my welfare, and everything for their sexual appetites. I guess "young boy" was on the menu. That's okay, they got theirs too. Of my mother, I heard nothing. My grandmother had no knowledge of her, nor record of my birth. Her last contact with my father had been years before I was born—she said he'd come looking for a loan.

Frank brushed up against my leg. I bent down and scratched beneath the grey's chin—a move that always brought the same pleased results—"Let me get straightened out, buddy, then we'll get you some breakfast."

I brushed my teeth in the shower—the water cold and hard— *I knew a man that claimed to have brushed his morning mouth with Comet—a trick, he said, that removed the filth of the evening. I had the cleanser, but I'd be fucked if I had the willingness to give it a shot. Besides, Frank didn't care if my breath smelled like shit—it's the missed meals that created bother, not the stink*—I toweled off and got dressed.

I fed Frank and then cleaned the house—my leather jacket I transferred to the bedroom where I hung it with reverence on the bedpost.

There's something about leather, man—it's like armor—armor for dudes who aren't afraid to take a punch—or turn a blade. I'm telling you, I can feel so fucking vulnerable at times—prey to the world, but then I slide my arms into that coat—the weight, cool heavy on my shoulders—I become invincible—untouchable—unbowed. I become me.

My knife was still in the pocket of my dirty pants. I fished it out and clicked the trigger—the hardened steel shown bright red streaks in the early afternoon sun.

Fuck, I hope that kid isn't gonna be a bitch about me teasing him with the blade. Oh well—if the cops do get involved, I'll just plead "mutual combat"—I was...defending myself—terrified actually. Ha!

I washed the boy's blood off the knife and then dried it with my shirt. I blew air into the switchblade's mechanism to keep the water from fouling the gears. I spoke to the blade.

"Piss and blood, my good man—there's nothing like a warm pirate's bath."

"Mr. Chance?"

A voice called from the doorway.

I turned to see a young brunette woman standing in my entryway.

Abigail Dupree—the shipping heiress. There wasn't a local gossip rag or newspaper that hadn't featured her face—and her good deeds. She was the Sweet Virgin Mary of caviar chomping society girls—young and pretty, but not my style. I prefer women with mileage—hard edges, loose morals—although her daddy's money was extremely attractive. And you know what, Baby, when a woman like this comes to see a man like me, she usually has nowhere else to go, and...if she has nowhere else to go...she'll probably do anything to stay.

"How the fuck did you get in here?"

She took a step back—"The door was unlocked. I thought this was an office."

"It is an office"—I laid my knife on the kitchen counter—"a residential office—appointment only, and it's a bit early for business."

"It's one o'clock."

"Yeah well"—I pushed my hair away from my eyes— "crime does sleep, eh?"

"Crime?" She flashed concern.

"Yeah, solving crimes and shit and high-profile business dealings getting all...worked out and stuff. What the fuck do you think we do here?"

Her gaze made quick work of my room—which, I admit, does look a bit like a ringmaster's suite—vintage carnival posters crowd peacock blue walls, red leather furniture, and above my desk an angry boar's head. I guess you could say that the room doesn't really say, "Detective," if anything—and I'm being quite hard on myself here, you could call it "childish and disturbed," but then I'd tell you to go fuck yourself.

I adjusted my slacks and waved her in—"How can I help you?"

She stepped deeper into the office as Frank strolled like feline royalty into the room—he eyed the door to the outside world.

"Well, I'm here because I—"

"—Hey! You wanna get the fucking door before Frank gets out. You should know better, lady."

She closed the door, but paid no attention to my little man.

Well, what do you know—according to Chekov she's only somewhat civilized. Sure, she might be kind to the downtrodden, but that tiara-wearing-savior-of-the-world bullshit just took a backseat to her feline indifference.

I offered her a chair and took my place behind my desk. I opened a cedar box and removed a short Cuban cigar, which I held beneath my nose. I inhaled its sweetly dark scent before I placed it in my mouth. For a moment I forgot she was there.

"Mr. Chance, my name is Abigail—"

"—I know who you are—what do you want?"

If she was offended, she didn't show it. You can't let these society types get up on you—treat 'em like trash, let 'em feel your disdain. My grandmother held no love for the idle, entitled rich.

"He told me that you could be rude, and that I probably shouldn't come alone."

"Who told you? And what do you think I'm gonna do to you? Come alone? You think Frank and I are gonna double-team you before coffee? Come on."

"Mr. Burroughs—he told me that you could be...a bit rough."

"Burroughs? From the Sentinel?"

I knew him well—a straight shooter. Newspaper boys can be a real pain in the ass, but not that old man, he was true fatherly cool—a heavy-hitting, cigar-chomping icon of the old guard—good to me, as I was to him. Burroughs was more than all right—he was like family.

"Yes, Tom Burroughs, but he doesn't know why I'm here. I told him I have a friend who thinks her husband is cheating on her— he suggested you."

"Oh, is that what this is about? Your friend's man is getting his cock greased behind enemy lines?"

"Mr. Chance!"

"Take it easy, Abi—you don't mind if I call you Abi, do you? I'm just fucking around—having a bit of fun. It's too early to be uptight"—I sighed and clenched the cigar between my teeth— "Now...is it you or is it her?"

She began to cry—high society tears, drying before they could become uncouth and ruin her make-up.

"It's me. I got involved with someone that I shouldn't have. He was sweet at first—handsome and worldly—quick to laugh and polite—a real gentleman—not like those spoiled pretty boys from the yacht club. And there was an air of excitement about him—a midnight storm casually floating behind his eyes—and like a young girl, I thought adventure…not pain."

"And you were wrong, right? I've heard this story before. Tell me, does this…uh, sea prince have a name?"

"Yes, but he's no prince, Mr. Chance. His name is John Hawthorne—at least, that's what he told me."

"Hawthorne. He sounds like a fucking asshole. What's with you broads? Some creep shows up with a hint of danger and a romance novel name and you jump on the fuck-stick. Why don't you go screw a couple of Bob Smiths or a Bill Jones? Nobody ever got fucked over by a Bill or a Bob—or an Emmet—shit, I knew an Emmet once—he was a pastor out in the East End."

"Mr. Chance?"

"Yes?"

"Do you mind if I continue?"

"What the fuck? I'm trying to help."

Her hands looked soft, yet industrious, and as she sat, they busied themselves with her handbag.

"Go on, Baby, I'm listening."

"Anyway, it started with casual drinks and a couple of nights out—the usual get-to-know-each-other thing. We progressed to kissing and acting as lovers do, and it was wonderful, but then it began to get more adventurous—sex in public places—the car, the park—even in the alcove at my church—and believe me, Mr. Chance, I did not want to be caught"—she lowered her eyes—"But then, I began to feel out of control—almost as if our relationship was only based on those clandestine trysts. I asked him if, maybe, we could refrain from our 'wild times,' but he seemed disappointed...and frankly, I'd fallen in love and I was afraid I was going to lose him, so I gave in. And then, Mr. Chance, I did things that I'd never done before—things that I wouldn't have done...had I not been drinking."

"Yeah, I hear that."

She wrinkled her nose as she inhaled my alcoholic breath— "I bet you do."

"Look, Babe, I don't mean to make light of this, but I don't see a problem—and watch your fucking cheek. So, you got liquored up and cut loose a bit—I'm sure it wasn't the first time. And if you're so bent out of shape, I'd suggest a therapist, not a detective— unless you're looking for your virginity—or an orgasm that somehow got misplaced."

"It wasn't the sex—I mean, yes, that's part of it, but it's what he made me do—what he's making me do now"—she looked about the room as if making sure we were alone—"Mr. Chance, are you familiar with my father?"

Her father? I live in the harbor. There's not a truck that goes by without the name 'Dupree' on it—sure I know him—one of those fat cat right-wing assholes—waving the corporate flag and championing the right of the unborn fetus—no matter how it got in there or who it came from. I favor eugenics myself, but then again, if they had cut my old man's nuts when they realized what a violent anti-social cunt he was, I wouldn't be here.

I leaned forward in my chair and feigned concern—"Are you pregnant? Do you want me to find the father?"

"No. I mean, I don't think so...no. I want you to stop them."

"Stop who? Who the fuck is, 'them?' Look, lady, you aren't making any sense. Did this Hawthorne rip you off? Did he beat you? If he did, go to the police. I don't handle that kind of shit. I'm an investigator—not a cop."

"I can't go to the police—they have photos."

"Who has photos?"

The faucet of her tears resumed.

I let her cry as I wondered if I'd bought coffee and if I'd picked up my laundry—come to think of it, I can't remember if I dropped it off. Sometimes they can be real pricks over there…

Her tears slowed enough to let her speak.

"We'd been drinking. He'd invited a friend over…a man."

"Hang on a second"—I opened my desk drawer, turned on a small hidden voice recorder, and then I leaned back in my chair—"I wanna get this straight. I need the whole story—you spare me no detail. If you want me to get you out of this—whatever the fuck you think you're in, I need to know exactly what they got on you—and if you hold back—anything—anything at all, you could be withholding something that's crucial to you—do you understand?"

"Yes. I do. May I call you Arthur?"

"No, you may not. Why would I let you do that? You can call me Mr. Chance—now, spill it."

She leaned forward, lowered her voice, and for a moment, closed her eyes.

"We'd been drinking. He'd invited a friend over—a man that I'd never seen before. He was tall like you, but not as rugged or as abrasive as you are, and he was smartly dressed, but there was something about him that spoke of evil and darkness. Our visit was innocent at first—you know, laughing and chatting, nothing too serious, and then when the stranger stepped away for a moment, John pulled me close and began to kiss me—lightly at first, but then heavier, almost forceful…"

Her words trailed off as if she was seeking the strength to go further.

"Go on, you ain't damned yet. I'm still wondering why you're here."

"It's just that…um…"

"Look, you're wasting my time, Baby. Either get to it or get stepping. I want a coffee and a smoke—not a bunch of 'ums' and 'uhs' from some little rich bitch with an overactive libido."

"I'm trying, please."

"Then get to it."

"I will. It's just…hard."

Frank jumped onto the desk. Abigail made a move as if to push him to the floor.

"—You touch that fucking cat and I'll cut you—talk!"

"He kissed me…"

"—And you liked it."

"I'm not saying I didn't like it! I did—but then his friend…he came back, pulled up a chair, and sat down in front of us. He lit a cigarette and watched as John spread my legs. I won't lie to you, Mr. Chance, I *was* excited—and as I said, I had been drinking. I closed my eyes and let John's hands roam over me, and then…I felt another hand on my leg, and his friend said, 'that's the stuff, Johnny—real high-end ass.' And, I don't know if it was the alcohol or something else—it must have been something else, but I let them take me. I kept thinking that John wasn't going to let it go that far—he'd said he loved me. I remember looking to him, silently pleading, before his friend climbed on top of me, but he didn't stop him—if anything, there was pleasure on John's face as he watched his friend use me."

I stroked Frank's back and then I removed the unlit cigar from my mouth.

"Yeah, well I love a good fuck story as much as the next guy, but unless you got something else—or a cure for what's going on in my pants, we're done here."

"Mr. Chance, you wanted details and I'm giving them to you. My story ends with the three of us lying naked on the bed. John had mixed me a cocktail to 'shake off the shame.' I drank it, and that's the last I remember until I awoke at home—dressed in my evening clothes, lying on my bed."

"And now you want him punished for it?"

"No. I want you to listen. I said that 'my story' ended, not 'the story.' I needed a shower—as if that could wash off what I'd done, and I felt sore and slightly disoriented. I walked into the bathroom and I took off my clothes. They had drawn on me. In thick black marker, the words 'rich bitch' were written across my stomach—a term that you so flippantly expressed earlier, and my thighs were rudely adorned with bite marks—covered, Mr. Chance. I was bruised from knee to hip, and I had been used."

"Fuck."

"Yes, 'fucked.' And, if that were all, I wouldn't be here. I would've chalked it up to being an idiot; I would've taken my lumps and moved on, but that wasn't all. After I'd showered and dressed—as I was getting ready to leave, I found an envelope on the desk. It was addressed to: 'Your Highness.' I opened it and inside were photos and a note which read, 'Are you ready to play?'"

I couldn't help but smile—"Did you bring 'em?"

"The photos? Yes, and I brought something else too—you insensitive bastard."

She reached in her bag and pulled out a large envelope. She placed it on the desk before her. I reached for it, but she covered it with her hand.

"Look, Baby. I've been on the wrong end of a few bad nights myself, but to be honest with you, getting screwed by a couple of creeps—unless you weren't compliant—and I'm sorry, but nothing in your story says 'rape,' well, then, you were a willing participant. They'll say you asked for it."

"What?"

"Yeah, that's right, Doll. That's the way it is. Shit—a fucking shyster wouldn't even touch that. You got fucked up, you got fucked, and it sounds like you got dumped. Now, if you wanna kick me down a couple of grand, I'll be glad to do a number on him…"

"Mr. Chance, for someone who wants the whole story, you're sure not very good at listening"—she took a long slow breath—"Before I left the house that morning, I looked at those photos, and they sickened me."

She removed her hand from the envelope.

I picked it up and held it as I looked into her eyes.

Jesus, and they say I'm cold. This broad's eyes were devoid of pain—empty. Hold on, was that a flicker of...nah, nothing. I wonder if she even really gives a fuck.

I opened the envelope and pulled out the photos—four glossy 8x10s.

The first photo was a shot of Abigail tied to an almost vertical table with what looked to be leather straps and cuffs. She was naked, spread, and as she said, they had drawn on her. There were fresh bite marks and small evenly spaced drops of blood—as if they'd rolled a sharp spur up her legs. The shots were professional—well lit—not great composition, but good enough to get off on—the kind of smut your random degenerate hides beneath his mattress. I let my eyes traverse her body, starting at her feet—noticing every detail; bites, bruises, blood trails, words, and a few more bite marks on her breasts. There was a handprint on her throat—she'd been choked. Her lip was swollen and slightly bleeding, but her eyes—they were open and intent—*she was aware as they assaulted her.*

"I thought you said that you were out—that you didn't remember any of this."

"I was out. I swear to you. I don't remember anything!"

I flipped to the next photo—Abigail was on her hands and knees. She had a bridle in her mouth and a saddle on her back. Sitting astride her was a black dwarf with a cowboy hat—boots with spurs, and a whip—other than that, he was naked.

"Fucking, Paul."

"You know him?"—she grabbed for the photos. I held them close.

"Yeah, I know him. It's the midget, Paul. He's hooked up with the local porno king—Dick Heavy—a real creep."

"Porno?" Abigail's face paled.

"Yeah, this doesn't look good. Was there talk of a film?"

"A film?"

"Yeah, if Paul was there, they probably shot it. A fucking midget with a ten-inch cock—you've never seen anything like it"

I stifled a laugh as I saw the next photo—*Abigail, on her knees. Paul's large tool was stuffed into her mouth; her high society hands cradled his shaft and balls—again, her eyes, wide open.*

"Hang on"—I turned the photo towards her—"actually, you have."

Abigail was silent.

I flipped to the last—*what the fuck? It was the blonde in the black-on-black sedan. She wore a leather harness with a large "strap on" cock. She was engaged in Abigail's anus as Paul held a leash that was secured to Abi's neck.*

I put the photos back in the envelope, opened the desk drawer, and pulled out the small recorder. I turned it off.

"What's that?" said Abigail.

"It's a recorder. I was gonna use it against you."

"Against me? Why?"

"Why not? You fucking come in here—telling me some random sex story, and what do I know? Maybe you're fucking with me—or you're just some rich nut cruising alleys for a rough trade fuck to get back at Daddy. I was listening to your bullshit and then I thought, 'Fuck it. Tape it and make her fuck you to get it back.' But then, I saw those photos and…"

"And you thought I was too pathetic to even blackmail? Are you kidding me?" Her tears ran free again—"A guy like you thinks I'm too dirty to fuck?"

"No, Babe, it's not like that. I saw those photos and I felt for you. I couldn't do it."

"Because I've been used?"

"Nah"—I got up and walked around the desk. I put my hands on her shoulders—"look, I'm sorry, Abi. I'll nose around, check out your Hawthorne. Maybe I'll hear something."

"Do you think I'm dirty, Arthur?"

"Well...if you are, it's okay by me. I like dirty"—I put my hand on her inner thigh and then moved it up between her legs, "and I like used"— I undid the buttons of her pants and slid them off her hips—"clean girls are for squares. I like a woman that likes to fuck."

She leaned into me as I dropped my slacks and pushed her back onto the desk.

"Do you have protection?" she said.

"Yeah—I've got a knife on the counter."

CHAPTER THREE—COFFEE BLACK

She didn't fuck like a rich girl. Most high-end bitches act like their pussy is an oyster on a silver platter—like they're doing you a favor by letting you touch it—and maybe they are, but Abigail, she fucked like street trash—like she had something to prove and she was gonna use her body to do it. I like that in a woman, when they try to fuck you into believing.

The door closed behind Abigail, but her scent and the envelope lingered on my desk.

I pushed the photos to the side and shook out the remaining item—a Port Authority locker key—*The familiar orange plastic cap was in place, but someone had gone to the effort of grinding off the four engraved locker box numbers that normally adorn the head. Whoever altered this key, didn't want a person to accidentally stumble upon whatever was in that locker. I should've discussed it with Abi before she left, but after I shot my load, I lost interest.*

Frank brushed against my leg—"So, what do you think, Buddy—does the same hold true for you? Do you like to see 'em cum, and you like to see 'em go?"—I scratched his back—"You know, I don't think you've ever had a piece of pussy—have you?

You're not gay are you?"—Frank rolled onto his side and stretched long; I picked him up and kissed his stomach—"Ha! You can suck all the dick you like, little man. I support you…and your community."

I walked into the kitchen to brew a pot of coffee.

Whether your morning starts before the sun rises—or as it sets, a hot cup of the bitter black is resurrection to the dead. I could go without food for days—and I have, but hot coffee or vodka, a man cannot do without.

The cupboard was bare.

I opened the refrigerator and pulled out a past-its-prime tomato. It resembled a shrunken head. I put it back in the fridge and closed the door.

Fuck—I really need to get my shit together, and I do try—every Monday I turn over a new leaf, but by Tuesday, I'm already screwed. What was it last week? Oh yeah, keep the cupboards stocked and stop jerking off so much. I don't think I hit midnight before I fucked that up.

I picked up my knife from the counter and put it in the front pocket of my slacks. I retrieved my jacket and my wallet from the bedroom. I checked my funds—two twenties and two tens were neatly tucked within my grip—small change for a cold day.

The private detective business is not a lucrative trade, but I'm doing all right. My grandmother left me a large chunk of change—in trust, so I couldn't drain it—foresight, they call that. She was good people—took a lot of shit from me before I came around—kind, but man, was she firm—persistent with her love. After a nip or two and a few cold runaway evenings, I wised up. I guess the old broad softened the edges of my heart. I tell you though, I got no idea how such a compassionate woman had raised such a vile prick as my father. I guess it speaks more for nature rather than nurture—some men are just cunts.

I gave Frank a kiss and walked downstairs. My landlord, Mr. Matsudo, has a small service garage behind the building. I store my bike there. The locked popped without a hitch.

Matsudo was probably oiling that thing on the regular—meticulous, that's what he is, and hard. He's like a tick dug into the rich flesh of the harbor lords. They'd love getting their fat hands on this property, but the old warrior won't be bought. He honors his ancestors by hanging on to what the "patriots" try to steal. I don't know how he does it, man, but he's one of those cats that you'd hate to fight; they keep getting up, no matter how hard you knock 'em down, and if you're not willing to kill 'em, it's best not to even start. It's a losing battle with fucks like him.

I pulled open the doors and smiled at my baby—a '72 "police special."

I fucking love this bike, man. I picked her up at a city auction—got the companion white helmet too—one hundred percent legit. It must'a been wicked to be a cop when they rode horses like these. Imagine: there you are on the highway—bike roaring like a wild beast beneath you; you come upon a carload of unsuspecting lawbreakers—force 'em to the curb, tie up your stallion—march, knee high, black leather boots, clicking full power towards their car, and then wham! You break out the nightstick and bust their motherfucking heads—excellent!

I zipped up my leather and put on my goggles.
I took the long way through the harbor—filling my lungs with the cool early afternoon air. I exhaled the alcohol of last night's debauch, and the pores of my skin dripped 80 proof pain. There was a coffee shop on the edge of the arts district—an oasis of the hot and bitter—*I'm not a fan of the hipster vibe or the $2 a cup coffee, but when your favorite diner is closed, and you need a fix, well, as they say, any sauce in a storm.*

The shop smelled like burnt Columbian roast and swap meet incense. There was amateur artwork on the walls—local color and positive slogans—*I bet you didn't know that a good day was your choice, and that thankful people were happy people. Christ. I'd like to put it to the author of that shit, really turn up the heat and see when his good attitude disintegrates. I don't think it'd take much. As for me, I'll be happy when the fucking diner is open.*

The clerk was a young, pink haired punkette with a plaid bondage skirt and a see-through t-shirt with no bra—grating voice, nice little tits.

"Welcome to Nietzsche's. What can I get started for you?"

"You can start and finish a large black coffee—unless you're thinking of doing yourself in."

I wondered if she'd ever been tied up before—if she knew who Nietzsche was, and if the skirt was meant for show or business.

She smiled—the rubber bands on her teeth matched her hair.

"Ugh," I groaned to myself, "you're a fucking creep, man."

"Did you say something?"

"Yeah. I said, where's the tip can."

"That's not what I heard"—she set my black coffee on the counter—"do you have a problem with me or something?"

"How old are you?"

"I'm sixteen."

"Then no, I don't have a problem."

"What if I said I was eighteen? Would you have a problem then?"

"What the fuck?"—I took a step back and checked for a camera—"are you a cop?"

"Of course I'm not a cop"—she tossed me a come-fuck-me smile—"and you're not the first creepy old man that's tried to hit on me—lucky for you, I like creeps." She pulled a lip gloss from her pocket and slathered it on nice and thick.

"Listen up, little girl—"

"My name is Jenny."

"No, your name is, little girl. If you were eighteen or even seventeen point five, I'd drag you in the back—tie you up with those fucking bullshit bondage straps, and fuck the braces off your teeth. But, as it is, I think you should watch your fucking mouth before some old creep—who doesn't have my integrity, comes strolling in here and puts you in a position that you don't wanna be in."

I reached for my coffee. She covered my hand with hers—sparkly pink nail polish and a kitten tattoo resided on smooth teen skin. I inhaled her perfume and unwillingly steeled in my slacks.

"First sip?" she asked.

She picked up my coffee and placed her mouth over the small opening in the lid—she made a loud sucking sound.

"Gimme my fucking drink"—I grabbed the cup from her hands—glossy pink lip prints soiled the rim.

"I'm just putting a little sugar on it, Daddy."

"Yeah, well fuck your sugar, Sweetie"—I turned towards the door as the girl snickered behind my back.

As I walked outside, a red Corvette Stingray jumped the curb and narrowly missed me. I quick stepped back, licked the spilt coffee off my hand, and waited for the driver to step out—somebody was gonna catch a beating.

Fucking Dick Heavy, man—the local porno king—a movie star...that is, if your celluloid galaxy was populated with greasy blonde pompadours, velour jumpsuits, and lubricating jellies.

"Hey, Chance—feeling sorry about the near miss, man. How's it hanging?"

"It's gonna be hanging hard when I beat your fucking ass, Dick."

I knew Heavy, and he knew me. Our very limited relationship ran neither hot nor cold, but, I had no trouble cranking up the heat on that creeping cock merchant.

"Come on, Arthur Baby, I didn't see you, man—you must have been sleuthing in the shadows"—he pantomimed a phantom creep.

I set my coffee on the hood of his Corvette—"How 'bout I kick you in the cunt, then maybe you could sleuth up some ice for that fucking thing?"

I was known for my willingness to get physical. Heavy was known for his junk. The crotch of his tracksuit looked like it was stuffed with an octopus.

He put his hand over the tightly stretched velour.

"Come on, Chance. I'm sorry, dude. I didn't see you. I'll make it up to you, man."

"Yeah, and what are you gonna do for me? You and that little asshat, Paul are gonna scratch my back? Or maybe, he sucks my dick as you do my shoulders?"

"Come on, Arthur—don't go hard on little Paul—he's all right."

"Yeah, and you're all right too, right?"—I picked up my coffee and took a sip—it was already cold. I spit it on the pavement—"You got something for me?"

Heavy unconsciously handled his crotch—"Fuck yeah, now we're talking, Baby. I can stir you up some trim, man"—he put his eyes on the coffee shop door—"I got my peepers on some real fresh meat—like right off the bone, dude. I'll kick you down."

"If you're talking about that underage piece of fluff in there, I prefer my women, to be women—you're not fucking that, are you?"—*Jealousy and righteousness inflamed my clenched fist.*

"No, no, no, man," said Heavy, "I'm not fucking; I'm farming, brother—planting seeds—grooming."

I forced down my cold coffee and tossed the empty cup at him. He caught it and saw the lip gloss. He smiled and licked the rim—"Oh, oh. Does Mr. Chance got a thing for that baby girl?"

"You're lucky I don't have a thing for fucking you up. You owe me, asshole"—I drug my boot down the side of Heavy's

Corvette as I saddled my bike and pulled away —"Have a good day, cocksucker—it's your choice."

I swung out to the Coast Road. Saint's Point was in the distance. There was a monastery on the hills above—*A ride out would do me good.*

CHAPTER FOUR—A DRINKING PROBLEM

My grandmother used to bring me to the Point. You can see the city from here and the wild coast to the north. She sought the comfort of the monastery, and I sought the comfort of the cliffs. I wasn't a fan of her God—if He was so great, why did she need to return here week after week—especially in her last days when her soft breath exhaled in pain with each small step. My life has no place for God. I prefer the reality of chaos—the roll of the dice.

I parked my bike near the monastery road and walked to the cliff's edge.

The rocks that I'd sat on as a young boy hadn't changed—but then again, neither had my belief in the evil that coursed through man—self-sacrifice and honor, love and compassion; these were not the go-to traits of humankind—they were anomalies in a system of wickedness.

Years after my grandmother had died, I came here to sit, and in the forced quiet of my repose, I heard the small voice of an animal crying in the bushes. The kitten couldn't have been more than a few weeks old. He was covered in dirt, his fur matted—a small grey skeleton close to death. I tucked the boy inside my jacket and carried him to the city. Frank was my grandmother's last gift to me. When the veterinarian had suggested putting the kitten down, I offered the same to him—"If the cat dies, so do you." You'd be surprised what miracles the medical professionals can deliver when they've received the proper motivation.

I looked down—the rocks and a quick end lay a few hundred feet below me—*I thought of jumping—as I always do, but then I slowly backed away. One day I'll do it—after Frank passes, but not yet. He needs me.*

When I was a teen—shit, and well into my twenties, my grandmother insisted that I continue to see a therapist, and I did—lots of them—mainly to appease her, but, sometimes I enjoyed talking about myself—wondering how I worked. One time this "doctor," a real creepy fucker with a bad hair piece, he told me that my thoughts of suicide—my reckless sexual behavior, and my alcoholism had all stemmed from my abuse as a child. Ha! No shit, genius—and you went to school for that, huh?

I picked up a small stone and bounced it in my hand. Its edges were smooth, aerodynamically sound, perfect. I imagined throwing it at a passing car—*Bullseye—I should've been a ball player.*

Sometimes I wonder what it would look like to not check yourself—to act on any desire or whim, to do 'what thou wilt.' I could've pounded that little coffee bar chick—why not, she was sexy...and fucking willing too. What makes it wrong—because it's law—man's law? And if so, what makes me any different than Heavy—you don't think he's gonna fuck her? He's probably pounding on that little ass right now. And that Abigail, Jesus—there's something wrong there, she's worried about 'looking bad,' but then she hops onto my desk and spreads her ass like a pro. Am I the only one with fucking morals around here? I'll tell you, man, I could do without reflection—it's my only weakness—this small little voice whispering in my ear. Sometimes I wish it would just shut the fuck up.

    I rode back to the city.

    As I cruised past The Nest, I saw T. Terry standing by his car—a highland green '68 Ford Mustang. I rode up behind him and revved the bike. He wasn't pleased.

    "Fucking Arthur, man."

    "Fucking what, dude?"

    "Fucking what? Are you kidding me? Stab anybody today?"

    "Come on, don't get so bent out of shape. I was just fucking around—was he hurt?"

    "Was he hurt? You cut the fuck out of him! Little bitch called the cops. I had Lemke and that other fuck—the new guy—what's his name?"

    "Roberts?"

    "Yeah, fucking Lemke and Roberts grilling my fucking customers—searching for the 'assailant.'"

    "Did they uh…"

    "—No, but as far as I'm concerned, you owe me two bottles of Chivas and an eighth of blow. And speaking of booze—you need to lay the fuck off. I thought you were sober."

    "I am sober."

    "Fuckin-a, Chance, if that's sober…ugh. I like you, Arthur—you're a good guy when you're off the shit, but you can't handle your sauce. You need to get it together—give it a rest. I'm not saying quit forever, but…you know."

    I admired my bike as his admonishment washed over me and into the gutter. A fucking drug dealer telling me I got a problem? Really? He's lucky I have better manners. I don't give a fuck what he does—unless it encroaches on me.

    "Hey, why don't you come down tonight? I got a sweet little trio coming in—jazz, you like that stuff, yeah?"

    "I don't know, man. Yeah, I dig it, but…they any good?"

"Good? They're fucking great. You know Harlan Keys—it's him and a couple of session cats. I'll get you a booth in the back. You can drink all the soda you like. I'll keep an eye on you."

"Harlan, huh? Yeah, he is the shit. One night I heard him do a great take on an old late fall track. It was real nice, real smooth—the kind of jam that takes you out of this world—you know. One time he and I got into a car—I think we were with Fast Eddie and…what's that other dude's name, anyway, we headed down to the uh…the uh—what's that place at the uh…"

"Ha! You're losing me, man. Come sober, Chance—it'll be a good groove—maybe a couple of ladies…and hey, leave the knife at home, all right?"

I smiled—*Of course he forgave me*—"You got my word on it, Brother. Sober and unarmed—it'll be a first."

Fuck, sober and unarmed? Is there a redundancy there? I usually arm myself with a few shots before I stand naked before the world—the blade, that's just protection for those that get beyond the haze of alcohol on my perimeter. Sober? God, there's been many a Monday when I set down that drink. Shit, I've quit lots of things— lots of times, but I did it without knowing I couldn't. It's easy to quit when you aren't aware of how much you need it. But when you know you gotta problem, and you've tried to stop before and failed, the quitting gets that much harder.

On the way home I circled the local liquor store three or four times before I stopped.

There's an argument that habitually runs inside my head— two voices. One says, "You need help, Arthur. You went too far last time. You could've killed someone," and the other voice says, "It wasn't that bad. You were just getting loose. You over-reacted on that whole sober thing. And one drink won't hurt."—I bought a fifth of vodka—*As I made my purchase, I pretended as if I wasn't there—*

I looked away when I gave the clerk my cash. I know it sounds crazy, but if I somehow distance myself, emotionally, from the bottle, it kinda absolves me from the act.

I garaged the bike and climbed the stairs to my office—one long step at a time. The bottle felt heavy in my hand. It was 6pm, and I hadn't had a drink since the night before. I was feeling a touch lightheaded—a sip or two would do me good.

"Frank! I'm home."

I sat the vodka on a shelf, picked up the locker key from my desk, and I lay down on the couch—still sober. Frank jumped on top of me.

"Hey, buddy. Guess where I went today—your old stomping grounds, the cliffs."

The grey burrowed between the cushions of the sofa. He turned and popped his head out.

"Ha! That's how I found you—those big ol' eyes of yours. You're a lucky fucker."

I put my head next to Frank and fell asleep.

I woke at 9pm and washed my face. I still hadn't had a drink since last night—nor had I eaten anything since yesterday afternoon. I gave Frank a small tin of tuna, and for myself, I took a bread-and-butter sandwich and a cookie—just one—I'm trying to cut back. The recently purchased vodka was where I left it—alone on the shelf. I strapped on my leather and walked out.

For a moment, I stood before the garage—keys in hand—ready to roll, but then I lost faith in my ability to stay sober and I decided to walk.

I'd promised myself that I'd never ride drunk again—except in emergencies. The last time I got it on before riding, I pulled a "wet and reckless"—spent a couple of hours racing around the harbor with my siren on, pulling over big rigs, and attempting to stop a twenty-car locomotive. I would've done it to, if the fucking police hadn't of fucked me over. I gave 'em my I'm-on-your-team bullshit, but it didn't go well with the arresting officers—neither did my resistance to their offer of a ride downtown. I didn't mind the beating—that comes with the territory, but it did take me a few days to get released, and Frank didn't get fed. He was pissed as fuck when I got home—a week of the cold fur shoulder and a well-placed turd on my bed before he decided to let it go—I didn't blame him. I wonder if my grandmother thought of my occasional incompetence and instability when she protected my inheritance—hmm, I guess she didn't have any faith in me either.

The goon at the door let me in without a word or a hassle. T. Terry must have told him I was coming. I was gonna offer a quick word of apology, but the big oaf gave me entrance with a simple head nod. There was no reason to complicate things.

You know, when I got one or two in me—I'm the man—I can do no wrong—the world is mine. But tonight, without so much as a drop on my tongue—almost 24-hours sober, I skulked into this club as if I had something to hide—a weak shadow of myself. This was gonna be a long uncomfortable evening.

I could smell the alcohol in the air—fresh and stale.

"What the fuck, Chance! You came"—T. Terry gave me a friendly frisk—"and unarmed—a man of his word."

"—Get the fuck off me."

"Just fucking with you, man. Come on."

He led the way to a small booth in the back. It was dark—red leatherette seating with a round Formica table.

The trio was on. They were playing, 'Sanctuary'—one of my favorites. Harlan had found himself a pretty good horn player—not Miles, but then again, who is?

I called toward the band—"Hey! Keep it tight!"

Harlan looked up and smiled.

T. Terry smelled the air, searching for my lying breath—"I said sober!"

"I am sober, you fuck. I'm trying to loosen up."

"Well, not too loose, okay? Let me get you something"—he waved over a waitress.

She was stacked—dressed like she'd crawled out of a harem, and she bounced on his call.

"Hi, Baby, how's my man?"

He ignored her too familiar greeting—*he was probably fucking her, but she was still just a hired hand.*

"Let me get my friend here a…uh…a what? What do you want, a Shirley Temple?"

I didn't look the waitress in the eyes—*I was embarrassed—a hard charger like myself ordering a soda pop. I wanted to pop T. Terry in the mouth*—"Just give me a fucking Coke, okay—no ice"—*there, that sounded tough. Yeah, I drink sodas, Baby—straight up…Jesus.*

T. Terry rubbed the waitress' ass. She leaned into it. "You keep 'em coming, Babe—anything he wants."

Yeah, sure, anything I want—they never mean that—motherfucker's got no idea what my anything is, and if he did, he'd know they don't carry it.

The waitress took her ass, her tits, and my drink order to the bar. Terry sat next to me and leaned close—"I got shit to do, but I'll check in on you—you hungry?"—he picked up a greasy menu card—the plastic edges dog-eared and torn—"The kitchen just closed, but I could see if they got something laying around."

"Nah, I'm okay—I just ate. I'll be fine with my soda pop and a pacifier."

"It's not that bad, Chance. Lighten up—lots of people don't drink."

"—Lots of people don't have to."

He gave me a light punch to the shoulder, and then he went about his business.

The crowd wasn't bad for a Sunday—mellow—nobody getting loose or starting shit. Terry was doing all right—the house was usually full, and on slow nights the cocaine sales made up for the lack of heads.

"Here's your soda"—the waitress set the drink on the table—a soggy Crow's Nest napkin placed beneath it.

I put my hand around the glass—"I'm taking it easy tonight."

She leaned forward—a loose tit practically dipped into my drink. Her breath was bad.

"What's it look like when you're taking it hard?"

"Thick, like your breath"—I turned my eyes to the band and set to my beverage.

The waitress, oblivious to my insult, bowed out—"When you want another, just wave. I'm all yours."

After the sixth or seventh coke, I had to piss. I left the table and made my way through a room full of pretentious, squared up, motherfuckers—sipping fancy whiskey drinks, and talking low-key sophistication as they listened to music that they probably didn't understand—*I'll tell you, man, you give me a couple of cocktails, and I'd show these bitches what's up.*

"Excuse me, asshole. You wanna watch it?"

I'd stumbled into a well-dressed blonde—*last night's drunken vision—the girl from the black-on-black sedan.*

"I'm sorry, Babe."

"You should be."

She gave me the shoulder, and I grabbed her arm. She turned on me—"Hey, what gives? First you walk all over me, then you assault me."

"No, it's not like that, Doll. Let me get you a drink to make it better—heal the hurt, so to speak."

She raised the glass in her hand—"I'm all filled up, cowboy."

She began to walk away, and then she looked down at the fresh black scuff-marks on her clean white boots. She held up sharp—braced me—"What are you, the school bully—you step on a girl's feet because you're too shy to say, 'hello'?"

"The bully? No. Don't you remember me"—I ran my hand across my jawline—"from last night…?"

"Last night? You're fucking dreaming, guy."

"No. I saw you—a black sedan on Cannery?"

She took a drink as she avoided my eyes—"The bum? Standing in the doorway? You clean up well for a hobo."

"I'm not a bum. I was walking home and uh—"

"—You saw me get slapped? And now, you think you can walk all over me and pick up the pieces. Is that it?"

"The pieces? No, I was just trying to say…I'm…you know what…fuck it—sorry I abused you."

I let it go, turned toward the restroom—her voice teased the back of my neck.

"Oh, so you're a bully and a bitch? A strong woman gives you a little source, and you crawl off?"

I squared her up and pushed back—"Are you out of your fucking mind?"

"No. I'm not, but I am thirsty. Why don't you act like a gentleman and spruce me up?" She handed a passing waitress her glass as she grabbed my arm—"What do you say?"

"I say, where's your beau, the tough guy that let you have it?"

"My beau? What decade did you crawl out of? If you're referring to 'him,' it was a one-time thing, and tonight I'm solo… at least for now."

"Well, if you'd like to have a drink, I've got a table in the back. We can cuddle-up tight, and I'll keep you primed"—*the seven cokes were knocking inpatient on my pipe*—"I'll be back in a minute. It's the empty booth near the bar."

"Where are you going?"

"I've got business in the restroom."

"And you're not inviting me?"

"Huh?"

"To the Men's room"—she grabbed my ass—"jeez, you are slow."

I snatched her hand and gave her wrist an almost painful twist—"Yeah, I'm slow…and you're too fast."

When I returned to my table, the blonde was seated and arguing with the waitress.

"This is a private booth, girly—it's taken."

"I know it is…by me."

I walked up and put an obsessively washed hand on the waitress' back—"It's all right, Baby, she's with me."

"Great—so I guess you're both drinking sodas?"

The waitress laughed. I didn't.

"She's having whatever the fuck she wants."

The blonde smiled at the server—"I'll take a Mai Tai, grandma."

"You better watch your fucking mouth, Blondie."

I jokingly put my fists up—"And you better watch yours, sugar tits. How 'bout I give you a little smack?"

Terry hustled to the table.

"Chance, what the fuck, man? Are you hassling my staff?"

"No way, dude. I'm good—sober and trying to entertain."

I sat down and put my arm around the blonde. The waitress was having none of it. "He's being a dick, Terry."

"A dick? What are you fucking doing—just serve 'em and shut up."

"Terry, I…"

He slapped her on the ass. "Hit it!"

The waitress forgot her hurt, cooed, and hightailed it to the bar. Terry stuck his hand out to the blonde.

"I'm T. Terry, this is my place…and this is my man"—he gave me a nod.

The blonde returned the pleasantry—delicate fingers and a diamond watch.

"I'm Nikki. Your man, huh? Do you own him, or can I rent him for an hour?"

"You can have him for free for all I care, but you better keep him sober—I gotta get."

"Keep you sober? Do you have a drinking problem?"

"Fuck no. Do I look like I got a drinking problem? I'm taking it easy—watching the band—relaxing."

The waitress came back with our drinks. I got a napkin beneath my soda pop; the blonde's Mai Tai splashed the table.

"Hey!"—Nikki settled her drink—"what the hell, you slob."

The waitress made a hasty exit.

I investigated Nikki's cocktail. It looked suspicious— "What's with the vegetables?"

"The vegetables? It's a pineapple slice, lime, and a couple of cherries. Are you kidding?"

"I don't like anybody swimming in my glass except the booze—and maybe a small ice cube—if I'm feeling fancy."

"You sure you don't have a drinking problem?"

I picked up my cola and gave it a sip—"Yep, no problem."

She cradled her glass—"This isn't really a drink anyway, it's more like candy"—she dipped her finger in the cocktail and rubbed it on her lips—"wanna taste?"

I leaned over and gently kissed her. Her lips were sweet, slightly tart, and delicious.

"Wow. How could you get drunk off something like that?"

"Drunk? Who wants to get drunk?"

"It's the point of the beverage, my dear—drink, drank, drunk. You know how it goes."

"Well, maybe if you drank these, you'd have more control—here"—she pushed her glass my way—"have a sip."

A sip...fuck—you know, sometimes there's a moment before you do something—something possibly life changing—for the good or bad, and in that small space, you pause and say, should I? And every fucking time I say—why not?

I lifted her drink—tossed the umbrella to the ground and spat that worthless lime slice onto the floor. I took a very in-control gulp of her "candy."

"Mmmm"—I smacked my lips—"that is nice. Let's get a another"—I waved the waitress over—"We're gonna need two more of these."

"T. Terry said soda"—the waitress looked for the club owner, but he was nowhere to be seen.

I pulled out my wallet and laid two twenties on the table.

"Yeah, sodas were free, but if I wanted a couple of these"—I gestured to the drink—"I'd have to pay for 'em. Now if you wouldn't mind...adios."

I pulled Nikki close.

"Fuckin bitch, man. She's fucking the owner, and now she thinks she can fuck over the patrons"—I pounded the rest of Nikki's drink and then looked to the bar to make sure the waitress was on it. She was.

"Wow," said Nikki, "look at you."

I kissed her neck and gently bit her ear—"And look at you."

We were about seven or eight drinks in before T. Terry returned. I'd inadvertently tripped a woman as she'd walked to the toilet, punched her defending man in the face, dumped a large glass of water on the waitress' head, and told her to go brush her teeth. T. Terry came to the table as we were on our way out.

"Chance, what the fuck? Where are you going?"

"We're stepping out, my brother"—I grabbed a random drink off a table and polished it off.

I'd never felt better as I put my hand on the small of Nikki's back and steered her towards the door.

Outside the club, I pulled her into my arms and kissed her as if we'd been in bed for hours—she kissed me back, in kind.

"And what now, Arthur?"

"I was thinking a walk to the pier. Have you been there before?"

"And what if I have?"

I kissed her shoulder and followed with a gentle bite—"A man can only hope."

She grabbed my hand and led the way.

The pier was the local Lovers' Lane for the adventurous, uninhibited, and overtly degenerate, late-night crowd—a transient population who favored the exhibitionist's fare. I guess if you didn't mind getting splinters in your knees, it was a great place to go down on someone— 'grab your tweezers, lovers. It's party time.'

We walked down a corridor of wooden plank blowjobs and creosote-soaked copulations. I pushed her against a piling and slid my hand under her skirt. She wasn't wearing panties. She spread her legs as I unbuttoned my slacks. Her perfume wrapped its subtle arms around me and pulled me in. She leaned her head back. I bit her neck—feeding for a moment—slightly breaking the skin. The head of my cock was against her, and then…she abruptly pushed me away—"Hang on, Baby."

"Hang on? What are you doing? I'm clean—let's do this."

She reached for her handbag—*it clashed with her boots.*

"Oh, fuck that noise"—I held my hard cock in my hand—"this is a fucking piece of art, Baby. I'm not putting a cover on it."

"You're an idiot"—she pulled a small blue vial from her

bag—"I like it raw…and you're gonna love this."

She unscrewed the cap, and I took the vial from her hand.

"To drink?"

"Yeah, Baby. Giddy-up."

I downed the liquid and stifled a retch—"Fuck, that's nasty."

She dropped to her knees and touched the head of my cock to her lips—"Yes I am, Romeo. Yes I am."

CHAPTER FIVE—JAILBIRDS DO SING

I couldn't get comfortable. A foghorn blew louder than it should have. The sound of the ocean and a truck stalling out in my living room was overwhelming. I was wet. I rolled over and attempted to pull the blanket around me, but there was no blanket. Discomfort forced open my eyes. I was lying on a railroad track—my head on a cold steel rail.

I sat up. My mind was slow to follow—"Fuck."

I knew where I was—the old train depot on Terminal, but not how I got there. I'd pissed myself—nothing strange there, but at least I was still dressed. That was a plus. My knuckles were raw, and my right eye swollen—possibly black. There were a few workmen in the distance, but they paid me no mind. To them, I was just another dreg living on the dirt.

I stood up and swayed from side to side before I gained my balance. From the look of the sun, it was early. I was a half-mile from home. I stumbled in that direction.

You know, it's not the first time that I've come to like this, as a matter of fact, I'm used to it. Some after-the-party wake-ups are worse than others, but they're all bad. I've never come out of a black-out doing anything good, and 'fuck' is always the first word on my lips.

After a couple of blocks, my head cleared, and I had no noticeably ill effects. I sought my own counsel.

"Okay, so I did T. Terry's and the blonde—what was her fucking name...Nikki, yeah that's right; a couple of drinks—nothing too bad, we went out on the pier to fuck...did we fuck? I don't think I fucked her. I remember her mouth, her lipstick—God, she had great lips. I think I got her number."

I checked my pockets—except for my wallet, they were empty—"Fuck! I lost my fucking keys? God damn it!"

I picked up the pace for home—Frank was gonna be pissed.

I had a spare key but I hid it somewhere special, and I can't remember where. I wasn't about to break the front glass again. I knocked on Mr. Matsudo's door. The old man opened it, but said nothing—he didn't have to; his eyes did the talking—disgust.

"Hey...uh, good morning, Mr. M. I'm sorry for bothering you, but could you let me into my place?"

"You were too loud last night."

"I wasn't even home." *My tone reflected my annoyance at another unsatisfied customer..*

"If you weren't home, then who in the hell was stomping on the floor? I told you before—too fucking loud for me."

"I'm sorry, I was loud. I wasn't home or...I don't know, maybe..."

"You don't know if you're home?"

"Yeah, okay, I was. I was home, and too loud. I'm sorry. Can you please just let me in?"

"What happened to the other key—the one before?"

"I lost it."

The old man shook his head. He reached for a ring of keys on a hook by the door—"At least you didn't break the glass."

I held out my hand.

"What's that for?" he said.

"The key."

"No fucking way—doesn't-even-know-if-he's-home guy. I'll let you in."

Mr. Matsudo took a slow climb up the stairs. I followed. The old man put the key in the lock and opened the door. My place had been ransacked.

"Frank!"

The cat was nowhere to be seen.

"Frank!"

Two middle-aged men entered the building and ascended the stairs—they carried badges—Detectives Roberts and Lemke.

"Arthur Chance?"

I ran into the bedroom, the bathroom—the kitchen— "Frank!"

"Arthur Chance."

I ran back to the bedroom.

"Arthur!"

I turned to see Detective Roberts in the doorway—Lemke stood behind him.

"Help me find my fucking cat, man!"—I shouldered Roberts as I pushed my way into the foyer —"He's fucking out, dude. Help me!"

"Lemke, grab him!"

Detective Lemke grabbed me around the waist and the two of us tumbled down the stairs. Roberts pursued. At the bottom of the landing, Detective Roberts swung—hard, heavy blows. I returned fire as I scrambled to get free.

"Let me get my fucking cat!"

Lemke got a handcuff on my left wrist. I put a knee into his balls. I fought for the door to the street.

Roberts screamed like a bitch—"Fucking Tase him, Lemke! Shoot the motherfucker!"

"I want my fucking cat. I'll do anything. I did it, fuck, I did it—just let me get Frank." I rose to my hands and knees.

Lemke backed away, and Roberts kicked me in the neck—lights out.

When I woke, I was in a cell at the substation.

Someone had done a number on my ribs and my left hip was killing me—probably from bouncing down that fucking stairway. The skin on my neck was raw—fucking pricks, man.

I stood and pressed my face against the bars—"Hey! I'm up. Hello?"—there was no answer—"Hey! Come on!"

In a nearby cell, a giant of a man crawled from his bunk and spat at me—"Shut the fuck up!"

I ignored him—"Hey! Lemke—Roberts! Let's go, man!"

"Hey, you crazy fuck, I said shut up!"

"Roberts! Come on, dude!"

"You motherfucker!"

A door down the hallway opened. I heard hard shoes stepping proud along the corridor. Roberts appeared at the bars.

"Look who's awake, the fucking cat lover."

The giant pressed his issue—"Shut him the fuck up, officer."

Roberts stroked his revolver.

I paced before the bars—"Let me out or get me to a fucking phone. I got a call coming, asshole."

Roberts shook his head—"Do you know why you're here?"

"Yeah, the boy—now give me a phone."

"The boy? There ain't no fucking boy, scumbag. You're being held on suspicion of murder."

"What? Fuck you. Give me my fucking call. I need to check on Frank."

"You out with a blonde last night—Nikki Graves, you know her?"

"Nope. Never heard of her. Give me my fucking call."

"She turned up dead. You were seen—murdered."

"I don't give a fuck about her! Lemke!"

"Officer, shut him the fuck up!"

"You shut the fuck up. Give me my fucking call, asshole! Frank!"

"Are you still going on about that cat?"—Roberts laughed—"He's dead. Your little kitty went bye-bye. He got himself all run over by a big, mean police car—bump, bump. Don't you worry about Little Frank—he's gone."

"No. You fucking prick—if you laid a fucking hand on him."

"He's dead, scumbag—courtesy of Goodyear."

I felt as if I'd been drugged, like the conversation between Roberts and I had shifted into slow motion.

I sat down on my bunk.

My sweet little boy was dead.

Two uniformed officers appeared in the hallway. The cell across from mine was opened, and the large, angry detainee was brought before my bars.

"Unlock it," said Roberts.

They unlocked my gate. The giant stepped inside. The cell door was locked behind him. I didn't move. The two policemen walked away. A door down the hall opened and closed.

Roberts smiled at the giant—"Shut him up."

The large man towered before me, but I remained seated—my hands tight gripped the metal rail of my bunk. The giant advanced—"You fucking punk ass bitch. I'm gonna do you."

With both feet, I kicked the beast between the legs—a fucking bullseye crotch shot. As the man doubled over, I jumped from my bunk and fired a vicious well-placed uppercut beneath his chin—teeth broke—lip split. The giant fell back and hit his head on the low metal toilet of the cell. I stomped on his throat, his face, his hands, his chest—anywhere I could, I kicked. I stomped him into near non-existence—blood splattered my slacks.

"ROBERTS! WHAT THE FUCK!" Lemke was at the cell—"Are you fucking kidding me? What's the matter with you?"

From the phone on the wall, Lemke called for assistance. The giant was breathing, but only just so.

Roberts stood frustrated before the bars—his cell house muscle thrashed. He glared at me as he spoke to Lemke. "You want to tell me what's up?"

"We got a call from downtown—the Chief said, 'let him walk.'"

"You got to be fucking kidding me—this piece of shit? We've got him on resisting and assault and possibly murder—not to mention this"—he looked at the unconscious giant. "Is he breathing?"

I said nothing.

"He's out," said Lemke, "suspicion—still, yeah, but as for now, he's walking."

The two uniformed officers returned. They unlocked my cell—Roberts stepped behind Lemke as they escorted me out.

"Hey," he called after me, "don't leave town, asshole. We'll be by."

I caught a cab home.

Frank was all I had. I hoped they hadn't left his body in the street.

When I stepped out, I stiffed the driver. His complaints were nothing but smoke—*The poor prick should've known nothing was coming when he saw my eyes—loss is universal.*

I stepped out and saw Mr. Matsudo standing at the side of the building. Frank's body was cradled in his arms. I began to cry.

"Hey, Arthur, do you ever let him get sunshine?" Frank lifted his head and stretched his neck—"You should take him outside more. He likes it."

"Little fucker. Where was he?"

I walked toward the pair and held out my hands; the grey jumped into the high grass—he rolled onto his back.

"He was here. I went back to get a hammer, and he was in the grass, chewing on a rat—you owe me for new stair paint and a broken rail"—Frank licked his paw and stretched in the sun. Matsudo bent down and scratched behind his ears—"Were your friends the ones that messed up your place?"

"Fuck. I forgot about that. No, I don't think so. Do you remember what time it was when you heard the noise?"

"It was late—after twelve. I was going to go up, but…you know how you get when you've been drinking."

"It's a good thing you didn't—who knows who or what you might'a run into…"

"Yeah, who knows, but you don't even know if it was you or not. The door wasn't broke. They had a key."

I thanked Matsudo again, picked up Frank, and went upstairs. I put my nose close to Frank's mouth and smelled his breath.

"Rat, huh? How was it?"

He didn't reply.

CHAPTER SIX—DINNER DATE

It was hard to believe that it wasn't me who wrecked the place—I mean, that was my M.O.—get hammered, black-out, come to in a fucked up house, and clean it up—but...fuck...that's the trouble with black-outs—you see; when you pass out, brain and body are both down, but when you black-out, the body wanders off on its own and the brain stays behind. God knows what the fuck I've done when I wasn't there.

I sat Frank down and got to work—starting with my bedroom. I folded my clothes and put them back in the drawers. The closet wasn't too bad—the shirts and slacks were still hanging, but my shoes were tossed about. I pulled up the carpet in the closet's left corner and lifted a small floorboard. A snub-nose .38 was as I left it—lightly oiled and wrapped in a silk scarf—a small box of ammo sat beside it.

I remember when I bought that gun—$40 bucks off a junkie looking to get well. I don't, as a rule, buy shit like that —you never know who might'a had it or what they'd done with it—you can tie yourself to a murder weapon without ever knowing. But when I saw that Colt—that short barrel and walnut handle, it was like *seeing a photo of my old man. A gun like that had done him, and I wanted a piece of it. I know, it's what he'd call sentimental bullshit, but some kids get their father's watch, I got a gun that could've killed him.*

I held the gun in my hand, and then as my father before me, I placed the barrel in my mouth.

I wonder what that motherfucker was thinking as that bullet tore through his brain—surely, if anything, not regret.

I returned the gun and replaced the board and the carpet.

I straightened the bedroom and moved on to the bathroom. Frank's litter box had been upturned—grey, coarse sand covered the floor. He stood by, curiously upset.

"It's like having piss on the toilet seat, huh, buddy? Fucking savages."

I grabbed a dustpan and a broom from the rear balcony. There was unbleached flour coating the kitchen floor.

What the fuck were they—or I, or whoever the fuck, looking for? Cat litter and flour, who'd hide shit in there?

I kicked Frank out of the bathroom and then I swept up the cat litter and dumped it back in the box. As I bent over, my earring fell and sank into the sand. My sense of humor was surprisingly still intact.

"Hey, Frankie! Go get me a fucking metal detector, huh."

As I said it, I remembered the time that I'd lost my keys on the beach—an old man had used his detector to find them—it cost me a twenty for a tip.

I pushed the plastic litter box with my shoe.

"Was I was looking for my keys? Yeah, that's what it was. I came home fucked up—wanted more booze, so I made up my mind to head back out, but I couldn't find my keys so I panicked, thrashed the place, and left without 'em. Jesus—I gotta stop drinking, man."

I hit the kitchen—used the dustpan and the broom to sweep up the flour. I straightened the cupboards and closed the refrigerator door—the over-due tomato hadn't been disturbed. I moved towards the living room, but then—*fuck, there they were—on my pink kitchenette, my fucking keys—sitting right on top—plain sight.*

"Okay, I'm out of my fucking mind. Did I tear the whole fucking place apart for nothing? They're right here—IN PLAIN FUCKING SIGHT? I'M LOSING IT!"

Frank—concerned about the disturbance, entered the kitchen. He jumped onto the table. I pulled it together.

"I'm sorry, buddy. I guess I couldn't find my keys. I sure hope I didn't upset you."

I walked into the living room and stared at the unopened bottle of vodka sitting on the shelf. I took it in my hand—felt its weight—twisted the cap—the paper cover tore as I opened it, and then, I slowly put the bottle back on the shelf. Clarity rose simultaneously in my mind.

"Wait a minute, Frank. There ain't no fucking way I was here—blacked out, and this bottle stayed unopened. No fucking way. That isn't me. I didn't wreck this place"—I looked down at my desk; the envelope that Abigail had given me was missing—"She did! *She* was searching for *her* key…fucking, Abigail, man. She must'a come here. She trashed it!"

A light knock fell upon the door—and then another, three in succession. I could see the shape of a woman's figure through the frosted glass.

I opened it.

"Hello, Arthur. Is this a bad time?"

I grabbed Abigail by the hair and pulled her inside—"You wanna fuck with me, bitch? You're fucking with the wrong one!"

She struggled against my grasp—grabbed my arm—I shook her loose and shoved her onto the couch—as she landed, the cushions and her body tumbled to the floor.

"You forget something? You better start talking."

"Arthur, stop this! I didn't do anything."

"You didn't come into my fucking house looking for your fucking package?"

"My package? What are you talking about? What package?"

"YOUR FUCKING ENVELOPE, YOU CRAZY BITCH!"

"Arthur, stop it!" She drew her legs beneath her—held one of the cushions as a shield against me as she sobbed.

"I ain't buying that shit—your bullshit tears. You came into my house to get that fucking key."

"Why would I? I gave it to you!"

"I'll tell you why"—I stood back and pointed at her as I spoke—"because uh...because you didn't want me uh..."

Her bravado returned as I stammered. She got to her feet— "You're an asshole! I didn't break into your house. I came here to see you. I wanted to talk..."

"I just thought, I...when I saw the envelope and the key gone, I thought you took 'em."

"Are you kidding me? And you call yourself a detective? If you're talking about the locker key, it's right there"—she pointed at the sofa—the cushions laying on the floor revealed the key that had laid beneath. I must have dropped it when I napped.

I tried to shake my head clear, but clarity evaded me. I was sure that she'd broken into the house, but then again, a few moments ago I'd thought it was me.

I picked up the key, walked behind my desk, reached up, and tucked it inside the boar's mouth.

"What are you doing?"

"I'm putting the key in his mouth."

"Why?"

"It's safe there."

"Safe from who, you crazy ass? The desk drawer isn't good enough? Take it down."

I know it was ridiculous, but I needed something to be in its rightful place—something concrete and controllable. It felt as if my mind was sliding across a wet train platform—the 5:15 speeding into the station, I needed it to stop.

"Just leave it, okay. I want it there. I want it right there."

I put the cushions back and sat down. I rubbed my hand through my hair as I closed my eyes—"Are you alright?"

"Other than having my hair yanked out by the roots, I'm fine. Are you?"

"No. I…I don't think I am."

I told Abigail what happened after she'd left—I left out the part about possibly fucking Nikki, but I went deep on my battle with the cops, thinking that Frank had died, and how I couldn't have gone on without my boy.

"I guess I came home in a black-out and fucked up my place, and then for some reason, I left again…but…the vodka…"

"It sounds like you had a horrible night…and although I rarely drink, I can imagine consuming all that liquor could make a man feel quite confused in the morning—if not for days."

She walked into the kitchen and returned with a glass of water. I took a small drink, and then I poured the remainder in a Creeping Charley that I kept near the window.

I got nothing against water, but water is for thirst. I'm upset, not parched. Booze is calming, celebratory, and energizing—I'm gonna have to enlighten her.

I walked over to the bookcase, retrieved the vodka, and filled my glass.

"Do you really think that's a good idea?"

I held the drink beneath my nose, took a deep breath— savored its restorative effects, and then I opened my mouth and poured it in—"Do you think it isn't?"

The shaking in my hands slowed—my head became clear. After another two fingers of the sauce, the grin of a chastised little boy crawled angelic upon my face—"Will you forgive me?"

"I don't know—I'm probably an idiot, but—don't ever lay a hand on me again. Do you hear me?"

"Okay."

"I'm serious. Do you hear me?"

"Yeah—I feel bad, I really do—I'm like the fucking asshole in a Hallmark movie, 'I'm sorry I hit you, Baby. You know I didn't mean to; no one loves you like I do'—fuck. I'm not an abuser—ever. I'm trying to be better."

"And this helps?"— She picked up my empty glass before I could refill it.

"Yeah"—I took the glass from her hand and poured another round—"almost every time."

She plucked a few loose hairs off her sweater and checked her look in the large gilded wall mirror—"Why did you think I took it?"

"I don't know. You ever quit something and changed your mind? I figured you regretted coming here—you felt embarrassed—what with the photos and all, so you came back and took 'em. I've quit shit a million times and...went back"—I stared at the glass in my hand—"you being remorseful seemed reasonable at the time."

"Do you know what I think? I think, you think too much."

I refilled my glass and tossed it down—"Think, think, drink. That's what they say."

I didn't resist as she put her arms around me.

She ran her fingers through my hair, and then she straightened her blouse—"You look like you could use a bite—come on, it'll be my treat"—she picked up her purse—"Do you mind if I freshen up first?"

"No. Go ahead—it's clean."

She walked into the bathroom, and after only a few moments she returned with an envelope and an 8x10 photo of herself in a compromising position—it was smeared with oily fingerprints.

"Are you fucking kidding me? You're jerking off to these?"

She tossed the photo at me—"Wow, look at me, Abigail, the super detective—the case of the missing envelope has been solved—it was the creep, in the lavatory, with a jar of coconut oil."

Shit. I'd forgot about that—my bathroom magazine rack. I don't usually jerk off on the toilet—I prefer the couch or the balcony, but I was sitting there—researching the shots and I got hard, so I tossed one off—and she was dead solid about that coconut oil—that's a smooth play, man—moisturizing and slick, easy to clean up.

I threw her a half-assed smile—"Research?"

"Give it to me."

I handed her the photo.

She placed it with the others—"I'm assuming you're done with these?"

"Unless you'd rather I held on to 'em for uh…more investigating?"

"No, thank you"—she glanced through the photos—"There's one missing."

"Fuck really?"

"Yes, really."

"I'll look around. I'm sure it'll turn up, and I'll get it to you."

"You might want to look under your mattress, you degenerate. I'll consider one photo on loan, but I'm burning the rest. You can hang on to the key—maybe you'll stop jerking off long enough to figure something out"—she stuffed the envelope in her purse—"Can we go now?"

"You're not sore?"

"Let's just say, I'm not going to call the police."

Gravatto's was an old school Italian place on the East Side. The maître d' greeted Abigail at the door.

"Ah, Ms. Dupree, it's a pleasure to have you back. Would you like your usual table?" He snapped his fingers at a nearby server.

"Not tonight, Carlo, something a little more private, please?"

His eyes traveled over me as if he was inspecting a plate of wilted greens—"I understand."

We were seated at a booth in the back. It was dark—candle lit—romantic—*I wished I hadn't pulled her hair so hard.*

I broke off a piece of bread and dipped it in the olive oil—"So, you wanted to talk?"

"Yes, but couldn't we just sit for a while—enjoy the evening?"

"It's not going away, Abi—we should get to it."

A waiter approached our table and greeted Abigail.

"Good evening, Tony," she said, "looks like a light crowd tonight."

"Lighter than usual, but the better to serve you, Miss Dupree—and what were we considering this evening—might I suggest a nice glass of wine as you decide?"

I picked up the menu—the letters were slightly out of focus.

"Please, Arthur, let me"—she took it from my hand and gave it to the waiter—"Bene, credo che ordineremo la specialita della casa"—she turned to me—"Would you like wine?"

"Wine is for winos, Abi"—I popped the bread into my mouth—"but yeah—whatever you'd like."

"Un bicchiere del vino migliore…e una vodka."

I laughed—"Thank you."

"Did you understand what I said? I'm impressed."

"I understood vodka—it's international."

The dinner was pleasant—the conversation uneventful. Abigail—supposedly seldom inebriated, matched me drink for drink.

I can't remember the last time I stepped out for dinner—it's usually Frank and I sitting around the table—chatting over tuna and liver. People make me nervous—I'm never sure what to say or how to act. I can't stand putting on a front, so I end up relaxing my guard and saying more than I should—over-sharing they call it. I prefer to stay home. But Abigail, she made it easy—small inconsequential words mixed with the house linguini and clams. If you took away the jail, the suspicion of murder, and my heavy hand, this'd be a nice first date.

She leaned toward me with a soft, slightly slurred voice.

"I met him at a party—it was Burroughs who introduced us. He was a reporter—you might have heard his name a few months ago, David Grayson."

"Grayson? The suicide?"

"Yes."

"From the Singing Bridge—I remember."

"Do I need to tell you what I think?"

"Let me guess—no suicide? Come on, Abi, they all say that. Look, mental illness is commonplace—suicide not as much, but—"

"—He was the one who gave me the key. He trusted me, and now I've become so paranoid that I believe our relationship was only based on my ability to help him."

"Your relationship? Were you fucking this dude?"

"I was dating him, and not long, but yes—we had been intimate."

"Do I need to get tested?"

"Do you need another drink? The asshole is returning."

I held my empty glass in the air and gave our waiter the nod—"I always need another—go on."

She drained her goblet—"He asked me if I could do him a favor—and, of course, I thought money or a connection, but he handed me that key."

"You didn't ask him what it was for—or why the numbers had been removed?"

"Of course, I did. He told me that he was working on a story, and that he'd placed information—a precaution he called it, in that locker. He said he removed the numbers for my benefit, 'give a precocious girl a key,' he said, 'and she's bound to use it.' It was all very light-hearted and, to be honest, I felt thrilled—as if I was a co-conspirator. I'm not sure if you're familiar with what the life of a society girl entails, but after a few thousand fundraisers, parties, and ribbon cutting ceremonies, a girl can get pretty bored."

"And you were seeking adventure—like you were with John Hawthorne?"

She poured herself another glass of wine—"Yes, I guess I was."

"And what about me? Is that what I am, another thrill, a dangerous, sexy rogue that you've fallen head over heels for?"

She blushed—"I never said sexy."

The waiter set my drink upon the table, and as I slid it towards myself, Abigail's eyes followed its path.

"Frankly, Arthur"—she lit a cigarette and sat as tall as her intoxication allowed—"the key was exciting for a week or two, and then I'd practically forgotten about it. I hadn't seen David in a while—he said he was busy, and so was I. And then one night—the night before he died, he called. He didn't sound any different than he had previously—he wasn't noticeably worried or depressed, and he asked me to give the key to Mr. Burroughs. I told him I would, he thanked me, and then he hung up. The next day, he was gone."

"And you think his lack of distress means that he didn't kill himself? Shit. I knew a guy who spent a week visiting loved ones—he drove all over town—in great spirits—talkative and engaging, and then he drove up to the mountains, stuck the barrel of a gun in his mouth, and blew his good mood all over the backset of his car."

"That's awful."

"That's the way it is..."—*I thought of the cliff's edge*—"you never know when someone is gonna take themselves out."

I took the cigarette from her hand, pulled a short puff—which I did not inhale, bounced a smoke ring off my untouched water glass, and then I dropped the butt in it.

Cigarettes are for cokeheads and convicts—lonely housewives and young boys trying to look cool. I'll smoke 'em if there's nothing else, but I prefer cigars. Cigars are for gentlemen.

Abigail gulped her wine. She grimaced.

"Is that why you drink?" she said.

"Why? Because I got no idea why people do what they do? I don't give a fuck about them. I drink because I prefer the comfort of alcohol—the reality of dreams. I drink because I'm chronically discontent."

"Arthur, you are pathetic—ha! I meant poetic."

"I prefer pathetic. Artists, my dear Abigail, are assholes"—I downed my drink and set the empty glass upside down on the table—"It's time to go, Baby—Daddy needs air."

I'd reached the apex of a drunkard's perfection—when the cheeks are tingly numb—the smile wide, and the demeanor that of the benevolent Lord—all was right in the world.

Abigail finished her wine, signed for the check, and then we headed toward the door. Before we stepped outside, she paused.

"I have to step away for a moment. I need to make a call."

"Jealous boyfriend?"

"Ha, of course not—I've got a possessive daddy. If you knew my father, then you'd know he loves his property, and I'm what he considers prime real estate. If you'd met me a year ago, it would've been dinner for four—you, my two handlers, and me. As it is, I've abandoned the bodyguards with the promise of constant check-ins and a good-little-girl attitude."

"I'm surprised he doesn't paint a tracking number on you."

"Do you think he hasn't?"—she giggled—"Don't wander off, I'll be right back."

After a short moment, she returned and we stepped into the evening.

"Miss Dupree?"

I turned toward the voice as a flash lit the night. Abigail grabbed my hand as a second blast erupted.

"Smile, Arthur."

"Huh?"

Another flash and the bright assault was over.

"Thanks, Miss Dupree." The photographer returned to his post.

I shook the momentary blindness from my eyes—"Do you ever punch 'em?"

Abigail drunkenly twirled, laughed, and stepped off the curb—"Punch them? Why would I ever? It's the life of a society girl, Arthur. You should try it. You'd make a cute debutant."

"And you should watch where the fuck you're going"—I grabbed her arm as a car narrowly missed her. I pulled her back onto the sidewalk—"Fucking amateur—you look like you've had enough."

She put her arms around me and leaned against my shoulder—her perfume—rich night jasmine, sang—"But I could always have more, right?"

I steadied her—"Yeah, I guess so. Why didn't you get the bottle to go?"

She put her finger to her lips and whispered, "Because I murdered it. Ha!"

We walked arm and arm in the night air. She still had a story to tell, but I was in no hurry.

I don't know what normal is, but this felt like it could be it—and you know, if this is normal, it isn't so bad.

A large city truck watered the streets and the lights of the shops were reflected onto the wisps of ocean fog that had come ashore. We'd walked farther than we'd planned—being lost in each other's company, but we weren't pressed to turn back. The street before us was awash in blue and red florescent light.

"Look Arthur, a fortune-teller. Please, can we?"

"Do you want a cold reading? I'll give you one. It's all bullshit—incense and strong perfume, some strange sour stew boiling on a stove in the back, a one-eyed housecat rubbing against your legs, and an old brunette with jumbo tits telling you that you're witty and secretly loved."

I deepened my voice and gave her my best Bela Lugosi— "You're going to meet a dark stranger…"

"Come on, Arthur; don't be a jerk"—she opened the door of the shop and pushed me inside.

It was as I said—minus the one-eyed cat. The woman that greeted us was an aging sex-kitten brunette with double D tits and a thick unnatural floral scent emanating from her flesh. I winked at Abigail. She took the lead—"We want to get our palms read, please."

The woman gestured to a matching pair of gaudy white chairs with pink tufted cushions. There was a table covered with a purple velvet cloth and for a centerpiece, a large crystal ball. The fortune-teller took her place in a gold painted chair reminiscent of a throne. My laugh was countered with an evil eye.

"You don't need to believe for me to read"—her eastern European accent was thick and slightly sexual in tone—"Your future is near—regardless of how inconsiderate you may be"—she reached for me—"Give me your hand."

I obliged.

She took a deep breath—"You were recently in fear for a loved one —and you drink too much."

I tried to pull my hand away, but she held tight.

It was fucking uncomfortable, like a too long hug from a caring stranger. I love fucking—thoroughly enjoy it, but I don't like being touched—especially like this.

With her free hand, she used her finger to trace a line on my palm. Satisfied, she finally released me and stared into my eyes.

"And how could you be good—a crusader, and yet, as vicious as they come"—she sat back in her chair—"Does that frighten you?"

"Lady, there's only two things that frighten me, and you ain't one. We came here for her, not me."

Abigail held out her hand.

The woman held her gaze on me—"I won't touch her palm. I knew as she entered, that there was nothing real to see. But tell me, young man; when you face yourself, will you be able to pull the trigger?"

Abigail squeezed my arm—"Arthur?"

I stood and reached for my wallet—"I told you, Abi— fucking bullshit. Let's go. What do we owe you?"

"Nothing. I wouldn't touch a cent from your hands."

"Well, isn't that a miracle"—I put my wallet back in my pocket and leaned over the crystal ball—my reflection stared back at me. "I'm gonna kill you, fucker."

I laughed as I turned away.

My reflection, upon our exit, remained.

"I fucking told you—crazy ass shit."

"But she wouldn't take your money."

"Yeah, she's on some fucking, psychic power trip. She's probably in there, right now, laughing about it"—I swung back into my Bela as I held an imaginary gun against my head—"You'll kill yourself! Ha! Fucking crazy bitch."

I grabbed Abi and gave her a tight squeeze—"Let's get the fuck out of here, Baby."

We caught a cab back to her car.

CHAPTER SEVEN—WHITE PRIVILEGE FAST CAR

The Aston Martin was fast, and Abigail, although still slightly buzzed, handled it well.

"Do you always drive drunk?" I asked.

"I'm not drunk."

"Do you always drive when you think you're not drunk?"

I put my hand between her legs and stroked her crotch. She pushed my arm away as she downshifted and took a hard turn— "Arthur, please!"—she smiled—"not while I'm cornering." She straightened the wheel, and as she pulled onto the motorway, she spread her legs and placed my hand back in her lap—"It's all yours, Baby."

She brought the car up to speed as we headed for the West Bay Bridge. The road was clear before us.

"Hey, Abi, do me a favor—get off on Orange."

"On Orange, why?"

"Just do it, okay?" I adjusted the rearview mirror to suit my need—"I wanna check something out."

She took the exit and glanced over her shoulder—"Are we being followed?"

"I don't know, maybe—go past this stop sign and pull over. I wanna see what they're gonna do."

"Arthur, this is exciting!"

"Exciting? Are you fucking crazy?"

The vehicle stopped behind us at the intersection and hit its brights—its occupant or occupants were obscured by the glare. They held idle at the crossing.

"Arthur?"

"Fuck, man. I don't know. I don't think it's a cop—unless they're fucking with us. Did you see a light on that roof?"

"No. I couldn't see anything."

"Me either. Fuck this, I'm getting out."

I stepped from the car and the strange vehicle lit it up in reverse. As I ran to Abi's door, they sped backwards down the street and cranked a hard turn around a corner.

"Get out, quick. Switch with me."

"No, I can drive."

"Fuck that, Abi, get out."

"I can drive"—she pulled the car forward and swung it around. I jumped in and we pursued.

"God damn it. What the fuck was that? They got the fucking lights in my eyes. I can't see shit."

We turned onto an empty boulevard. I scanned the side streets, but neither lights nor the car could be seen.

"Where the fuck are they? Keep going, Baby."

"I can't. The road ends."

"Shit. Fuck. Abi! Back up! Back-up!"

I could see the ramp leading up to the highway. A set of headlights heading south towards the harbor.

"How the fuck did we miss them? Come on, Baby. Hit it! Hit it!"

She pushed the pedal towards the floor, and the Aston devoured the road, barely missing the retaining wall as we climbed the ramp. Abigail swung onto the highway and opened it up—ninety, ninety-five, one hundred, one-ten. I couldn't help but smile. She merged into the fast lane with room to move—one-thirty, one thirty-five.

"Fuck, man. They're on it!"

Abigail took her foot off the gas.

"What are you fucking doing?"

"I can't."

"What?"

"The police are behind us."

"Oh, Fuck."

She made her way towards the shoulder and came to rest on the side of the highway. The police cruiser pulled behind us—red and blue lights flashing through our windows. They hit us with their address system.

"PLEASE CONTINUE ON THE SHOULDER TO THE NEXT EXIT."

Abigail turned off the car and undid her seatbelt—I put mine on.

"No, Babe. They want you to get off on the next off ramp—not here."

"I've never been pulled over. I don't know what to do."

"What?"

"DRIVER OF THE GREY CAR; PLEASE CONTINUE ON THE SHOULDER TO THE NEXT EXIT."

"I've never had a ticket"—Abigail put her belt back on and fired up the engine. She slowly pulled forward—"are they going to arrest us?"

"Are you white?"

"Does that matter?"

"They don't arrest rich, white girls in sports cars—unless they're drunk. Roll the windows down and don't breathe on him."

"What do I say?"

"Nothing—let me do the talking."

The officers approached the Aston. One walked to the back of the passenger side of the vehicle. The other made his way to Abigail's window.

"License and registration please."

I leaned over Abigail—*You gotta know how to talk to these dicks—nice and smooth, polite and willing—compliant*—"Is there a problem, officer?"

The cop bent down and hard flashed his light in my eyes — "Shut the fuck up. License and registration please."

Abigail handed him the documents.

"Abigail Dupree?" He politely positioned the light on her, and then again turned its harsh beam in my direction—he lit me, head to toe—"Are you okay, Miss Dupree?"

"Is she okay?"—*Fucking prick*—"She was speeding. What do you mean; is she okay?"

"Arthur. Stop it."

The officer nodded at his partner. The policeman standing in the back moved forward and opened my door.

"Would you exit the vehicle, sir?"

"Yeah, you got it, buddy. Let me uh, unfasten this belt first." I unbuckled and stepped out. I turned away from him and put my hands behind my back.

The officer called to his partner—"Martin?"

"I've got no idea, Paul. Cuff him if he wants it and walk him back."

Fuck—this is what you call power trip conditioning. How the fuck was I supposed to know that they didn't wanna arrest me? We were pulled over. I was asked to exit the vehicle—the hook-up always follows the exit. I was trying to be a good citizen—they should've recognized that.

I was cuffed and walked back to the cruiser. The lead officer continued with Abigail. I chatted my guy up—*sometimes the charm helps.* "She wasn't drinking, officer—I was, but it was only one or two. I told her to see what the car could do, but she was against it the whole time, I mean, I practically had to push her foot down with my foot—and it isn't like that car doesn't just shoot off on its own—look at the fucking engine in that thing, man, it...uh, it really is something."

He put me in the back of the car and shut the door.

You see, this is the kinda shit that I'm always talking about—the dialogue between the average street cop and the general public is a long way from hospitable and understanding. We should be in concert—a partnership of basic street morality. These boys in blue, they were supposed to be the people's militia.

From my rear seat confinement, I could see the conversation—the lead cop laughing as he spoke to Abigail. He offered her his hand, and then he stepped away from the car. As he came toward me, his smile became a frown.

"All right, asshole."

"Yes, sir. As I was trying to tell, Officer Paul there—it is Paul, right?"

"—Shut the fuck up. I don't know what trash like you is doing with Miss Dupree, but you should thank her. I'm sure if we ran your name, you'd light up like a Christmas tree. Isn't that right...uh?"

"Arthur."

"Yeah, Arthur. That's the only part of your story that's probably true. Get the fuck out of here."

I walked back to the Aston and climbed in—"Fucking hard-ons. What'd he write you for? Did he give you the whole thing?"

"Write me for?"

"The ticket, how much did he cite you for—miles over; one twenty, one thirty?"

"I didn't get a ticket. He gave me a warning—two of them actually; one to slow down…and one to ditch the creep."

I put my hand back in her lap—"Fucking, white privilege. It's people like you that give guys like me a bad name."

As I opened the front door, Frank rubbed against my leg. I picked up my sweet boy and set him on the kitchen table—fixed him a nice bowl of Chicken Treat.

"There you go, buddy. I know it's not your favorite, but if you have your favorite every day—it gets old, quick."

Frank, instead of diving into his meal, pushed at an empty drink glass with his head.

"Ha! You little fucker; is Daddy hungry? I swear to fuck, Abi. This little bastard knows more than you think he would."

I walked into the living room and returned with the almost empty bottle of vodka—*just enough for a late evening taste*—"Hmmm, I have my favorite every day, and I'm not bored. Maybe that's what he was trying to say—right, Babe?"

"Arthur!"

I walked into the bedroom—Abigail was lying on my bed—stripped down to a sheer bra and panties.

"A leopard skin bedspread? Really, Arthur, where do you find such things?"

"You don't gotta lie on it."

"I'm not saying I don't like it."

I grabbed her leg and pulled her off the bed.

"Hey! I was kidding! Come on!"

I led her into the living room and steered her onto the couch.

"We're not done, Abi. We need to talk."

She looked like a little girl that had just been told a holiday was cancelled. She held my hand—"I'm not sure where to begin, I—"

"Fuck that shit, Baby—just spill it—I'm fucking tired and I've had a long day."

"Okay—jeez, stop it; I brought him girls."

"Who, David?"

"No, of course not, I brought them to John. They were friends of mine—well, not really friends, acquaintances—they never knew what happened to them. He used them, like he used me."

She released my hand and went to that state I'd seen before—devoid of emotion—robotic. She sat back on the couch and stared almost blindly toward the wall as she spoke.

"When I was given those photos, I panicked—I had—everything to lose. Could you imagine—Abigail Dupree, heiress and philanthropist being passed about like some sleazy pornography girl? I was desperate—willing to do anything—and I did. John told me to come see him and to bring a friend. There's no shortage of women that try to cozy up to my money, so I picked one—a lesser-known hanger-on, and I asked her if she'd like to have dinner. Of course, she jumped on the offer. I picked her up at her place, and on the way to the supposed restaurant, I told her that we needed to make a stop—of course, she didn't argue. I took her up to John's—although I was unsure of what was going to happen. And at first, nothing—he was his usual charming self. We chatted as if I had never been bound or ridden by a dwarf—don't laugh, Arthur."

"Come on, that's funny."

"It's not. Grow up…let me finish. I saw John put something in her drink—green liquid from a small vial. She drank it as I sat frozen, terrified, wondering what was to happen, and at first it seemed as if it had no effect on her. She calmly went on in her boring little high-pitched voice about Greece and London and Paris, and then…she stopped talking, as if she wound down like a toy. It was then, that John approached her and told her to stand—she did. He told her to take her clothes off—she did. He told her to get on her knees and open her mouth, and she did. John unzipped his pants and pulled out his penis, and then…she did."

"Wait, you're telling me that that liquid had something to do with her sucking him off? Are you fucking kidding? Fucking,

Abigail—no drug does that—not that fast or that complete or…hold up, a vial? Did she remember what happened when she came to?"

"No, she was confused, like I was. I put her on my sofa, and when she woke in the morning, she had no idea of how she got there and no recollection of what we'd done to her."

"We?"

"Yes, I helped him."

"Helped?"

"I participated—are you enjoying this?"

"No! I'm trying to figure this out. Didn't he drug you too?"

"No, he didn't—not then."

"How do you know? If the drug works that quick and that complete, you could've been out without knowing."

"I wasn't. I remember everything—even the drive home; the traffic, the red lights—the clarity in her eyes and putting her to bed. I told her to close her eyes and she did. Although…there was something else."

"What's that?"

"Well, I'm almost embarrassed to say this—hard to imagine that under the circumstances, but on our way home, I asked her a question and she couldn't or wouldn't answer."

"What'd you ask her?"

"Come on, what's it matter?"

"What did you ask her?"

"I asked her what she really thought of me—there, yes, I know it's childish, but this girl is a notorious gossip, and I wondered what she was saying behind my back."

"And she didn't answer?"

"No. It was like, I could tell her to do things—anything, and she'd do it, but she couldn't think on her own or verbalize at all."

"Like a fucking zombie or something?" I stroked Abi's leg—"Fuck, man, I could sure use something like that—how many girls did you bring him—each one of 'em filmed?"

"None of them were."

"Huh?"

"He didn't film them—he used them, we used them."

"And that was all?"

"All?" She put her head in her hands—"I helped him rape four of my friends. I led them to be drugged and used. I participated. Isn't that enough?"

"Yes, of course that's enough…and I meant 'all' as in—you're not holding anything back—not that what you did wasn't terrible. I'll tell you, Abi, you're a real piece of work, but…I don't get it. What do those photos of you and Grayson's locker key have to do with each other? Why didn't you just give that key to Burroughs?"

"He's an old man, and…"

"—And so, what? A fucking key to a locker that you got no idea what it holds or where it is—and you said yourself it was no big deal. Why didn't you give Burroughs the key?"

"Because I don't trust him!"

"Why not?"

"Because I saw him speaking with John. They were standing on the outer promenade by the municipal pier. I almost pulled over, but then for some reason I didn't—call it a girl's intuition or just a hunch, but it felt strange."

"Okay, so he knows John—big deal."

"But he doesn't—or at least he acted as if he didn't. John and I bumped into Burroughs a day or two later at a downtown restaurant, and he was taken aback—not noticeably—at least not to your average girl, but it was to me. I live in a world of fake smiles and put-ons. I was taught by my father that when a person speaks to you, look for even the slightest eye twitch or change in their demeanor. Burroughs hugged me, and then he introduced himself to John, as if he didn't know him."

"But you had that key before you met John. Why hadn't you given it to Burroughs?"

"Because I wanted to see what David hid in that locker."

"And what was in it?"

"Nothing—I never found it. There are a thousand lockers in that terminal, and I hate to sound egotistical, but I'm known. I couldn't possibly try every locker without being noticed, besides, I found out that John wanted that key. The night before I came to you, I went to him. I waited outside his building and when he came out, I approached him. I demanded to know when this thing was going to stop—when he was going to release me, and he said, 'I'll stop when I get what I want.' I told him I'd done everything he'd wanted—given him all I had, and then he said, 'What about what David told you? When are you giving me that?' It was then that I realized that John appeared shortly after David's death, and that was no coincidence. I told him that David gave me nothing, but he was adamant. He thought that David must have told me something or given me something; and to get free, I was about to tell him about the key, but I didn't. I kept my mouth shut. John reached into his pocket and he pulled out one of those vials. He tapped it, and then he smiled and said, 'We'll know soon enough,' and he left."

"Any idea what he meant by that?"

"It was a threat—I think he planned on drugging me again."

I walked over to my desk, pulled from my drawer a small cigar, lit it, and then I sat quietly for a moment.

"Abi, why would you come to me if you didn't trust Burroughs?"

"I did trust him, for the information I asked for a private detective to follow a friend's cheating husband. I trusted him for that, and he gave me you."

"And you lied to him."

"Yes, I did."

"And the car that was following us earlier, you have no idea who that could be?"

"No. How could I?"

She was full of shit—a ramped up tale meant to convince a square that she was on the level—I've used it often; if you talk deep and detailed, it sounds legit.

I took a strong hit and sent the smoke up towards the old boar's head—for a minute it was as if the stuffed beast was breathing fire—"So, nothing that Burroughs knows would make him think that I was doing anything other than tailing your imaginary friend's husband."

"No, I don't think so."

"And you've told no one else about the photos or the key or…me up until tonight."

"I haven't"—she covered her mouth with the back of her—hand as she yawned—"Can we go to bed now?"

"Yeah, go on. I'll be there in a minute. I wanna get a couple more puffs off this before I dust it."

I didn't know what she was after, but she sure smelled nice, and God, was she willing.

CHAPTER EIGHT—OLD FRIENDS

It was 3am when she woke me. She was doing her best to be quiet, but I'm a light sleeper, and the kiss on my cheek was too much.

"Did you leave a hundred on the dresser?"

"Why?"

"Because you're treating me like a whore—dinner and a fuck, and then you sneak out while I'm snoozing. I feel used."

"Arthur—I paid for dinner."

I pulled her onto the bed and made love to her again. It was quick, but at least to me, satisfying—"There—now we're even. You can go home now."

Abigail laughed as she gathered her things—"Good night, Frank. You be a good boy."

It was kind of her to include my little man—maybe she wasn't all bad.

I listened as she walked down the stairs and fired up the Aston—the car's deep throaty engine engulfed the night air. I hoped it didn't wake Matsudo. I didn't need another lecture.

I heard Abigail pull away, and then, as she sped down the

street, another engine came to life. I jumped from the bed, but I was too slow to the window—I caught taillights speeding up Broadway.

So what, another fucking car is cruising the perimeter—all night long fuckers are tooling around here—it's a great place to get high. I need to stop assuming that every fucking car is some fiend out to get me. Okay, so we were followed, but they didn't tail us back here. I kept my eye on the rearview the whole way. There was no one eating our dust. Sometimes I can be so goddamn paranoid. You'd think I'd be better by now. I've gone over this shit—with a dozen different therapists, and still my first thought when a stranger reaches into his pocket is; he's coming out with a gun— motherfucker.

I thought about going back to sleep, but then I remembered the vodka—*It was borderline empty, but maybe, just enough for a small put-me-back-to-bed sip—a wee taste.*
I retrieved the bottle.
Frank settled himself on top of the bedspread—"You can get underneath if you want"—he gave the bottle a dirty look—"Suit yourself. You snobby little prick."
I tilted the vodka, and the spider at the bottom—the very last drop, crawled into my mouth—"Nighty-nite, Frankie—sleep tight."

I was standing on a cliff watching the waves below—the sea, an eerie dark green with blue florescent flashes of light. A car pulled up behind me—a black limousine with bright orange rims. I turned toward it. The driver's door opened, and a human-sized Frank stepped out. He was wearing my clothes—my beige slacks and my camel hair coat—in his hand my father's revolver. I reached in vain for my knife. The gun turned into a clear glass marble that he rolled across his fingers. "Arthur,"—Abigail's voice called from below— "Give me my boy." The sphere in Frank's hand was now a crystal ball, and as he approached, my reflection grew in size until it choked the light from the world. I stepped back, and then back again. The cliff gave way beneath me...

I rolled over and reached for Abigail, but I came up with a handful of Frank. He nipped my arm.

"God damn it, you vicious bastard!"

I flicked him with my finger. The grey shot off the bed.

"I hope you're good with a can opener—cause if you ain't, you're going hungry."

I put my slippers on—my "Man About Town" pajama bottoms, I folded and placed in the drawer.

Abigail had given me some shit about my choice in eveningwear, but I shut her up with a hand over her mouth and a set of cashmere handcuffs—courtesy the tie from my robe. I wonder what she's up to—shit, I got no way to reach her—I don't even got her fucking phone number—I guess round three will have to wait.

I looked to see if she'd left a note—she hadn't.

"She can play hard to get, Frankie, but I've already had her—and if she's waiting for me to call...good luck."

I did my best to forget her.

I put a bowl of food together for Frank, and then I set out to make coffee before I realized that the cupboard was still bare.

The phone rang.

I picked it up—"You missed me. I knew you would."

"Arthur? This is Detective Lemke."

I hung up.

The phone rang again.

I answered—"Are you calling to apologize? If not...fuck you."

"Arthur, we'd like to speak with you."

I hung up.

The phone rang again.

I answered—"You know, I'd love to keep this conversation going, but I'm all out of coffee, and you can fuck off."

I hung up.

The phone rang again, and again, and again.

This time I answered it in a feminine singsong voice—"Hello…"

"Arthur? It's Tom Burroughs."

"Who?"

"It's Tom Burroughs—did you forget me?"

"No, I uh…shit, I'm sorry. What's happening, Mr. B?"

"Well, we haven't talked in a while, and I was wondering if you'd like to get together for a cup and a smoke—you still smoke, don't you?"

"Yeah…sure."

"Are you okay? It's a little too early to be snookered, don't you think?"

"I thought you were the police."

"The police? Are you in trouble…wait, that's ridiculous, when aren't you in trouble? I've got business in the harbor, and if you haven't had breakfast yet, I thought we could meet at that little diner there—my dime. Are you in?"

"Yeah, of course I'm in"—there was a light breeze coming from the kitchen window—my bare ass was cold—"uh…when? I think I'm ready to go."

"Let's make it 10:30."

"PM? They close at two."

"Are you kidding? Breakfast, Arthur, 10:30am."

I looked at the clock on the wall. It was 9:15—*an hour that I rarely saw*—"Fuck—so this is what daybreak feels like, huh? I'll be there."

"Are you sure? You sound a bit—"

"No, I'm all right. I'll see you in an hour or so—thank you."

I showered and dressed. As I made ready to leave, the phone rang again. I answered.

"Arthur, we can do this the easy way or we can do it the hard way. We'd like you to come in for an interview—and bring your knife."

"Lemke, you seem to have caught me in a better mood. Leave that fucker, Roberts, at home, and I'll be glad to come in for a chat. And by the way, I haven't forgotten what he told me about Frank—you tell him that. Make sure he knows."

"What time will you be down?"

I hung up.

I was about to head out the door when I remembered my blade. I couldn't find it. I checked my jacket pockets, but then I realized that I hadn't brought it to dinner.

Fuck, am I slipping—wallet, jacket, knife—three things I rarely, if ever, travel without, and last night, I didn't think to bring the blade. I ain't scared, but when the mind starts going, and the basics of daily personal protection avoid you, you can't be far off from wearing tinfoil hats and shitting in the street.

I didn't panic, but as my search of the bedroom yielded no results, I became a bit more intense. The living room received the hard-core rifling treatment.

"Okay, this is getting fucking ridiculous, man. Where is that fucking knife?"

I went back to the kitchen and immediately I thought about the flour and the cat litter.

"Was I looking for my blade? God damn it—that's why my fucking keys were on the table. I wasn't looking for the keys; I was looking for my knife. Jesus, I don't know what the fuck was in that vile, but that shit fried my brain. I'm out of my fucking mind."

Frank jumped onto the counter and wailed.

"Stop it, buddy. I'm not speaking to you."

I left without straightening my place.

Lucky's Swill opened at 5am and supposedly closed at two, but when the cook-slash-owner got tired, he kicked out the patrons and went home.

I love the diner—the food is much better than the name suggests, and being waited on reminds me of my grandmother. I miss the old broad something awful. She used to let me make my own little menus. She'd be in the kitchen whipping up crepes or mush or some other tasty please-a-young-man concoction, and I'd be out at the table smoking and complaining about the poor service.

The lot was full as I pulled my bike near the front door. Burroughs' blue '40 Ford was parked in a handicap spot.

Fuck, I guess we're all getting older, huh?

I checked my look in the bike's small mirror—the hair was solid, a nice wind-blown fade.

I'm not a vain man; but it's nice to know you're looking good—"I'd fuck me" isn't that what the kids say these days?

Burroughs was standing in the diner's waiting area.

I didn't buy Abi's bullshit about Burroughs not being trustworthy. He'd never done me wrong. He'd been a friend to my grandmother—the only other person at her service besides the priest and me. When I was a teen, I wanted to be a reporter, just like Burroughs, but I'm not always good with the facts or the discipline it takes to be thorough. I'd rather just beat a story out of somebody rather than sitting around trying to piece it together–As a matter of note, the onetime Burroughs had asked me to help him out, that's exactly what I did—I extracted a story by force—he wasn't pleased.

"Arthur, you're looking quite…rugged."

"And you're looking more and more like Hitchcock, you old fuck. Let me see that cane."

Burroughs held his walking stick in a threatening manner—"I'll give you the cane, you little shit!"

I slid into a karate pose and cracked my knuckles— *á la— James Woo.*

"Are you kidding me?"—The question came from an attractive waitress with dyed red hair and a blue star tattooed below her left eye—"You've got some fucking nerve, Chance."

"Brooke!" The cook chastised her with her name. He waved at me with a stainless-steel spatula.

The redheaded waitress grabbed a menu and led us to a table for one. Burroughs was confused—"Miss?"

"Oh, that's right, there are two of you"—she steered us toward a booth—"normally, people with dogs eat out back." She went about her business.

I called after her as I followed her ass with my eyes—"And a couple coffees, yeah! No cream!"—I smiled at Burroughs—"Do you know she used to be a dominatrix?"

Burroughs looked over his shoulder and then quickly turned back—he'd made eye contact with the waitress as she stared viciously at our table.

"Jesus, Arthur. How do you know that?"

I picked up a fork and poked the back of my hand—"Let's just say I was exploring my submissive side."

"She's not going to mess with our food, is she?"

"Nah, maybe mine, but not yours—and, if she did, it wouldn't be the first time."

The waitress returned with two cups of pure Colombian brown. As she set my drink before me, she dipped her finger, two-knuckle deep, into the hot beverage.

She addressed Burroughs, "What would you like?"

"I think I'll have the #2 with the eggs over hard, please—and if you could, butter the toast all the way to the edges."

She picked up the menu and began to walk away.

"Miss," said Burroughs, "my companion, please."

"I know what he wants—grilled cheese on raisin, no orange slice, and a side of house potatoes with sour cream and jalapenos."

"And a dill pickle. Don't forget that."

"Sure thing, pal."

"You always were quite the ladies' man, Arthur—speaking of which, Abigail Dupree; have you seen her?"

I looked into his eyes before I answered—not long, just a quick peep to make sure that this was the same old Burroughs that I knew—a man that could be trusted and...I guess, loved—whatever that means.

"Yeah, she came to see me the other day…"

"About her friend's husband?"

"Yeah and…uh"

"—And you didn't believe a word of it."

"Well, at first yeah, but…hey, show down huh."

"Arthur, she's in trouble."

This wasn't like him—he wasn't this skittish, this quick. Burroughs was the kind of cat that you could sit with for hours and you'd still barely know he was there. Something wasn't right— maybe Abi was on to something.

"What did she tell you?"

"She didn't tell me much—boyfriend trouble."

"John?"

"Yeah, that was the name."

"Did she mention another?"

"No. Just him."

He stared into my eyes—that fucking x-ray vision depth that my grandmother used to pull on me—you know, when I'd fucked up and was too scared to come clean. She'd hold me in this net of intensity—and I couldn't look away; I had to fess up to escape.

"Arthur?"

"Yeah?"

"Arthur?"

"Fuck, man. What do you want? I told you she came to me— which is a fucking violation anyway—client detective privilege and all that shit—"

"What about David?"

"Who?"

"What did she tell you about him?"

"You're fucking out of line here. She told me Grayson—I

mean Hawthorne, and I said I'd check him out. Fuck. What do you want from me?"

"I want decency, Arthur"—he stood up—"and if you can't bring the truth, I've other places to be."

He dropped a twenty on the table, put on his hat, and grabbed his cane.

"You're fucking leaving? What are you doing?"

"I don't know what kind of game you're running, son—but I do know that you're running one. You disappoint me."

He turned his back.

"Fuck, I'm not running anything—I'm sitting here, with you, trying to get some fucking breakfast—come on, man."

He shook his head as he walked away.

When the waitress returned, she set both plates in front of me—"Wow, what a shock—you're dinning alone." She headed back toward the kitchen.

I called after her—"Hey, I want my fucking pickle!"

CHAPTER NINE—MISSING

You can never go wrong with a grilled cheese on raisin, especially when you add the dill pickle on the side—you've got your sweet, your salty, and a touch of tang to put you to rights; and when I'm feeling as if the world is going to shit—more so than the average day, I throw a root beer malt into the mix—heavy on the malt. My grandmother turned me on to that drink. It was a rough day; the courts had sent me to yet another therapist—a real touchy-feely emoter who was digging deep into discovery, and out of nowhere, as we were talking about my inability to keep my hands to myself, I could smell my father's sour breath and I could feel the smooth leather of his belt as he tightened it around my neck.

On the car ride home, my grandmother did her best to soothe me. She passed me a tissue—her white-gloved hand echoed kindness—"Arthur, no man is God. Humans can't see the infinite world—oh, we think we can—as you probably think you can today, but the reality is; man is too small to hold all the knowledge of the world in his mind—at best, he can only feel its pulse."

I wiped my runny nose on my sleeve—laid my head against the car window—the glass was beyond cool.

"You cannot judge what is good or bad. Your father was ill; his actions were those of a sick man. Don't despise him, pray for him."

I might not have prayed for him, but I prayed with him. I leaned over his dead body and said, "Thank you, Jesus."

I paid the bill and made my departure. Brooke followed me outside.

"So that's how it is huh?"

"How what is?"

"You don't call me; you act as if I'm nothing"—she put her hand on my shoulder—*grease, perfume, and a faint trace of coffee breath*—"How'd that pickle taste?"

"Come on, Brooke, you gonna fuck with me every time I come in?"

She puffed up her beehive hairdo, and with a crooked pinky finger, touched her lipstick—"Maybe you should have thought of that before you fucked me."

I laughed and blocked a slap that failed in connecting. I caught her arm and pinned it behind her back, pressed into her, and lightly bit her neck.

"Do you miss it?"—I whispered—"Tying me up? Whipping my ass before work? Telling me to stick it up pretty for you?" I put my knee between her legs and forced them open—I pushed until my thigh was against her crotch—"Do you miss waiting tables with my cum between your legs?"

I loosened my grip, and she wrenched away.

"From the look of your pants, you're the one that misses it— fuck you, cocksucker." She stormed into the restaurant as I fired up my bike—*Cocksucker, huh? Jesus, one time, and they never let you forget it.*

The substation was an old 1930s public works project—a construct of steel, concrete, and corruption. There was new talk of making it obsolete, but the Chief of Police was against it. I've always liked the look of this place, but it's a building that I've never walked into of my own volition. And I'm sure if the Chief is against its demise, it's solely based on his proclivity to station the dregs of his force here—a real, blue-coated horror show.

I crossed an intricate inlaid marble floor and came upon a large wooden counter framed with iron bars. The waiting area had two wooden pew style benches and a matched set of water fountains. I expected a sign over the left one to read "colored"—and it did look as if they'd removed a plaque of some sort, but they were now both "free game."

The officer behind the counter looked as if he was strung too tight for deskwork—his reddish-purple face and protruding belly said health-risk. I figured I'd push the issue. I put my manners aside and leaned heavy on the counter—I cranked the volume—"I'm here to see Lemke!"

The officer startled and knocked over his coffee —the brown tepid liquid ran off his desk and onto the floor. He pulled his paperwork away from the spill.

"Do you mean, Detective Lemke?"

"Look, pal, you wanna call him detective because you're part of some fucked up hierarchy of blue-gang bully boys climbing the ladder of authoritarian cocksuckers—you go right ahead. But you see, me, the average citizen—standing on this side of the bars— I don't gotta play that game, and I don't give a fuck how much time he's put in or what his badge says or how many of those little powdered donuts you can stack around his flesh nightstick—so why don't you go get me my man. Okay?"

The officer pushed his chair back—the rolling recliner slammed into a filing cabinet—for his size, he was fast to the window.

"Hey, scumbag, how 'bout I stack you on your ass?"

I laughed at his agitation—"In my ass, wearing that outfit? Yes, please—stack 'em up, officer!"

"You motherfucker!"

An office door opened, and Detective Lemke stepped out. He was holding a cup of coffee—#1 Dad inscribed on the cup. The desk cop stood down.

"Arthur"— Lemke opened the gate—"come on back."

"Well, look who it is"—I winked at the overweight desk officer—"Private First-Class Lemke. Good morning, corporal."

"I'm in no mood for your shit, Chance—we got a major missing person situation. Harris, bring Arthur a coffee, okay."

"Yes, sir."

"Ohh, a coffee would be nice—black and extra hot—and one of your little powdered donuts, please."

We walked down a corridor to a small room on the first floor—the number "2" was inscribed on the door in dark blue paint below a small glass window. I followed Lemke inside and was met by a metal table and two chairs. I was directed to a seat facing a ceiling-mounted camera.

"You know, this really isn't my best side."

"Do you think murder is funny, Arthur?"

"See, that's the thing—you guys keep talking about murder, but I've got no idea what the fuck you're going on about."

"Did you bring your knife?"

"And that, dear Lemke, is another thing. I haven't seen that blade in days."

"In days, meaning two or three"—Detective Lemke set the folder on the table and opened it to the first page—"is that when you assaulted Brian Harper?"

"Who?"

"Brian Harper, the young man that you had an altercation with on Saturday last."

"If you're referring to the gang of thugs that attacked me on the dance floor—yes, I had it then—thank God."

His gaze traveled over my scarred knuckles

and climbed to the old, jagged cut above my left eye.

"Would you like to tell me about the Jacobsen incident?"

"What the fuck does that gotta do with this?"

"Well, I'd say when you've previously been arrested for manslaughter—"

"—Arrested yes, convicted no! That motherfucker got what was coming to him—and I don't know what the fuck you got in your notes, but you should see that!"

"It's hard to control your anger, isn't it?"

"Ha! You smooth fucker—playing as if my passion for life is somehow a passion to kill. I'm doing you a favor just by coming in here, but if you don't wanna play nice—I'll go home."

Detective Lemke turned a page and sipped his coffee. "So, you went to The Crow's Nest on—"

"—And I got a cup coming too, right?"—I three tapped the desktop with my finger—"Let's put it right here."

"Yes, Arthur, you've got a cup coming, but if you're expecting prompt service after your earlier behavior, well…"

"Ha! Motherfucker, he's probably fixing it up!"—I sent a yell down the hallway—"JUMP TO IT, BIGBOY!"

"When did you last see Miss Graves?"

"Oh, that's right"—I sat tall and organized some imaginary papers on the desk—"all business—let me see…I last saw the uh, perpatress right before I might'a fucked her."

"So, you had intercourse with her?"

"Hold up, Lemke; as far as cops go, you're not a bad one, and I'm kinda on your team, so I don't mind coming over here and giving you some information, but that girl, Nikki Graves, she was just a random nightclub pick-up—I didn't even know her last name before Roberts gave it. We had a few drinks, some laughs, and then we walked out on the pier to fuck around—that's it, and to be completely honest, I must'a had two too many because I don't remember anything after that. And as for my knife, I'd left that at home, you can check that with T. Terry—he'll vouch for it."

"Yes, Mr. Terry did vouch for it. He also said that you were slightly agitated when you left."

"And he used those words, slightly agitated?"

"No, actually he said, that you had 'slipped into asshole and split with the blonde.' I took the liberty of translating."

"Ha!"

"So, what did Miss Graves do to upset you—did she rebuff your sexual advances, laugh at your...uh, equipment, what was it?"

"My equipment? Ha! If anything, she was the aggressor— she didn't upset me at all. I don't know about you, but when a gorgeous blonde is getting all flirty and close—rubbing up against you, well that isn't something to get upset over. And if you wanna see if there's anything to laugh about—in regard to my equipment, I'll flop it up here on the desk and you can fingerprint it."

"Speaking of prints, would you be willing to give me a set of yours?"

"My prints? How many fucking times have you rolled me?"

"I know it's an inconvenience, Arthur, and I appreciate your cooperation, but you see..."

"—You've got no fucking prints on me—nothing?"

"No, Arthur. I couldn't find anything."

"Ha! Well, let me see...I'm trying to remember if I've done any recent cat burglaries before I agree to your uh...."

"—Arthur, please."

"Yeah, fucking print me, man. I've got nothing to hide. Fucking clown shoes, dude. What kind of operation are you guys running down here?"

There was a knock on the door immediately followed by the desk officer entering the room. He set a paper cup—quarter-filled with coffee on the table in front of me. It was cold. He addressed Lemke—"They found the car."

"Was she in it?"

"No—empty—stripped."

Lemke thought for a moment—"Where was it?"

"The packing plant—all hell is breaking loose—more press than badges—I don't know how they got on it so soon."

"Okay," said Lemke, "—I'm almost done here."

Detective Lemke closed the folder as the desk officer stepped out.

"There is something," I said, "I saw her in a black sedan on Saturday night—she was being assaulted."

"Who, Abigail?"

"Abigail, why would you say that?"

"Oh, it's nothing. Abigail Dupree is missing. We found her car this afternoon. What about this sedan?"

I sat dead still, but my mind had run from the room, jumped on my bike, and tore up the town—Abigail? Missing?

"Arthur—you okay?"

"Yeah…I'm just, uh…"

I had to keep it together—what the fuck, man, I wasn't paranoid—I was right on about that car. Fuck, why didn't I walk her out?

"Arthur?"

"Yeah. I was trying to see if I could remember the plate on that sedan. I was walking home, and I saw the blonde and some cat arguing—he hit her. That's what led to me talking to her—that I'd seen it—are you done with me?"

"Did you see what he looked like—this man in the car? Could you describe him?"

"Nah, it was too dark"—I stood up—"I'm sorry that she was hurt or uh…killed—she seemed all right to me."

"Yeah, one more thing, Arthur—"

"Look, Lemke, I really gotta get going—I've got things to do, man."

"It'll just be a minute more, please, sit down."

I retook my seat, but it was now angled toward the door.

"You told me that you'd blacked-out, was it from the drinking or something else? If I recall, you'd said in your testimony in the Jacobsen case that you had—and tell me if I'm wrong, that you had 'blacked-out' and 'came to' as you were standing over his body."

"Yeah, that's what I said, but this wasn't like that. Saturday night I'd been drinking—too much. I wasn't threatened by anyone."

"Okay, Arthur. You can go"—he pointed at my untouched cup of coffee—"Do you want take that?"

His voice fell against my back as I left the room.

CHAPTER TEN—GUILTY

Arne Jacobsen was a real vicious fuck—a small time hood whose game was strong-arming mom-and-pop grocery stores, gas stations, and local businesses. He was nobody—no connections, no associates, and definitely short on heart. But when a 6'5 monster comes in and demands free goods and a few bills out of the till, you give it to him—connected or not. I didn't like it, but I guess the world needs bottom feeders too because he'd been around a while. Of the incident Lemke was going on about—the manslaughter; I was in the corner market, I'd grabbed a pack of chips, a can of tuna fish for Frank, and was just about to purchase my vodka when Arne walked in. I stood to the side and let him pass—a real ugly fucker with odor much worse than his bad skin—he had the kind of stink about him that a man gets when he goes past ripe—a cold, under-the-overpass reek. I stood against the wall, opened my chips, and I waited. I guess he didn't like it. Maybe he wanted privacy as he fleeced the place. He told me to get the fuck out. I didn't say anything. I walked up to the counter, set my chips and tuna down, and then I asked for a fifth of Popov—The little girl behind the register was scared—trembling, barely able to grab the booze. Her hands were shaking so fucking bad, and then she looked at me with the saddest set of brown eyes that I'd ever seen. It broke my fucking heart—this little baby-girl being scared like that. And at that moment, I decided that I wasn't gonna let anyone hurt her—let alone that fat fuck. I told her it was gonna be okay, and then I turned around—I was staring down the barrel of a gun. Now, as I said earlier, this clown's thing was intimidation, but on that day, he was slinging metal. Well, I put that fifth of vodka upside his head before his fat finger could squeeze the trigger. And maybe I should'a had a gun because that bottle to his head didn't do a fucking thing. He teed off on my face with that pistol—used it like a pair of brass knuckles, and he beat the living fuck out of me—took out two teeth and broke my fucking cheekbone—my brow. I went down, and then that fucking ape put a boot on my throat and there wasn't a fucking thing I could do about it. I was scared like I'd never been before—kicking and gasping. I was thinking, this is it—I'm dying, on my back, in a fucking liquor store, choked out by a size 15 Sears work-boot—un-fucking-acceptable. I got my hand on my blade—seconds before going out, and I dug that fucking knife into his leg, right behind his kneecap— I gave it all I had. He went down, and when he did, I got on top of him and I guess I blacked-out. Next thing I know, I'm standing over him and that little girl is screaming—her voice hoarse from terror, and Arne, he wasn't moving—twenty-three mortal wounds they told me—I took out his fucking eyes.

I hustled out to my bike, turned it over—intent to move, and then I realized, I didn't know where to go.

I didn't have Abigail's number and no idea who to call—it's not like I could just tool over to the Dupree plantation and knock on the front door—"Hey, Mr. D, I've been balling your little girl and I'd like to join in on the search"—shit, I'd sound like that junky that steals your shit and then helps you try and find it. They'd probably slap the cuffs on me. I could call Burroughs, but that breakfast chat hadn't gone so well. Fuck—man, this is a real drag. I'm drifting into

*sad puppy romance land with this chick and the straight shot is—I
don't know a fucking thing about her.*

I rode to the packing plant—*figured a quick look couldn't
hurt.* The police had the frontage road barricaded and a host of news
trucks were camped out front. I circled the block. On my way down
Canal, I slowed; there was Burroughs' Ford. And there he was—
standing next to a uniformed officer. As I passed, we made eye
contact—his face expressionless.

I split for home—hit the corner market on the way—got
myself a fortifier and made ready to wait.

*I'm not one of those cats that jump right to a doom and
gloom conclusion, but it didn't look good. I don't know why she left
my house that night, or even more so, why I even cared. I told myself
a long time ago that love was for suckers—it's a sign of weakness,
a way to get hurt, but I guess she slid through the cracks and trickled
into my heart—I was pretty undone.*

I put the bike in the garage and wiped it down. The salt air
played hell with the chrome—*sometimes the simple things—the
chop wood, carry water, actions of life are the best when the head
is wandering.* "Who's running the show," my grandma used to say,
"you or your mind?"

I climbed the stairs, and for a moment, my worry left me; a
large brown envelope was leaning against my door. I opened it—
photos.

"Fuck—this ain't good."

The first pic showed me fucking Nikki's mouth. She was on
her knees, and I had my hands on her head—pulling her hair. Her
face was bruised, and she was crying. The second photo—more of
the same, except this time she was tied to a chair—I had my knife
against her breast as I held my erect cock. The third—worse, she'd

been cut—sliced across her chest. I was smiling as I held one hand at her neck, choking her.

When I saw the fourth photo I retched.

I'd slit her throat.

I sat on the top step of the stairway and took a deep breath. This was no time for panic. I placed the photos into the envelope and closed the seal.

I had to get my shit together—I put myself into the now by verbalizing my present state—leaving emotion aside.

"I'm in the stairway of my apartment. I'm wearing a pair of black slacks and I have my favorite shirt on. I'm wearing pink socks—the right one has a small hole where my big toe is, and the left one seems to have slipped down around my ankle. My shoes are black wingtips—slightly scuffed. I loosely tie them, because when they're tight, they pinch. I can feel the carpet of the staircase through my pants and the air is slightly stuffy—mildewed."

I took a few deep breaths and then, a few more.

Panic can make even the worst of times, worse—it multiplies the problem by a thousand and disintegrates the solution. But what do you do when you are unknowingly a murderer? How do you hold tight, stay calm, when you're the problem? I got no one—I've marooned myself on an inner-city island of violence and drunkenness. I've got no family and no real friends—yeah Burroughs, but...he ain't even talking to me, and maybe Abigail, but where the fuck is she? My contacts with the outside world are, at best, superficial—yeah, I got Frank—Friday to my Caruso, but if anything, he's the master and I'm the servant, and now, it looks as if I'm one of the cannibals.

I stood and took another deep breath—inhaled, exhaled. I felt as if I was gonna pass out.

I left the vodka on the landing and walked downstairs to Matsudo's. I knocked, he answered.

"Arthur."

"Hey, Mr. M, did you happened to see the person who left this at my door?"

"She's too young for you."

I looked behind me as if someone was there.

"Who?"

"The girl that dropped that off"—Matsudo pointed at the envelope.

"Could you describe her?"

"She wasn't too bright. There are only two marked doors in this building, and one of them has your name on it. She knocked on mine."

"That doesn't tell me what she looks like."

"She had blue teeth and hair."

"Blue teeth?"

"She had blue rubber in her mouth—braces"—he thought for a moment—"and a tattoo."

"A lot of girls have tattoos these days."

"On her hand—a kitten."

"Did she say anything?"

"She asked if you lived here. I pointed upstairs, and then I watched her climb. She's too young for you."

I started to walk away, and then, with new purpose, I stopped.

"Hey, Mr. M? Could you do me a favor? I gotta go away for a few days, and I was wondering if you could watch my Frank?"

"Where are you going?"

"I'm on a case. I gotta see a client up north."

"You actually investigate?"

"Yeah, come on, man."

"I thought you just drank"—the old man smiled—"Is he a mess inside?"

"No, no way. He's a perfect little man; the best ever..." tears filled my eyes.

"Ha! You and that cat, Arthur—you love him too much—of course, bring him down whenever."

Frank met me at the door. I took the large grey into my arms and cradled him—but not too long. Frank was a good sport, as far as cats went—he allowed me to love him, then he wiggled out of my arms and walked off to attend to other business. I sat down on the floor.

What the fuck does that little coffee bitch got to do with those photos? Yeah, Matsudo said, blue not pink, but a kitten tattoo, it had to be her. I think I'll pay her a visit—if anything, I won't go out alone.

I stood up—albeit somewhat wobbly, kicked off my shoes and stripped off my clothes. I laid my shirt and pants neatly on the sofa; my pink socks went into the dirty laundry and my wingtips were returned to the closet. Naked, I cleaned Frank's litter box before I gave the whole place a full going over: I dusted, did the windows, vacuumed, and mopped the kitchen floor. The pantry I left untouched, but the inedible food in the refrigerator—specifically the over-ripe tomato got tossed. For a moment, I stopped and looked at my hands.

I've done some real fucked up shit in black-outs—came to embarrassed, ashamed, and swore to myself that I'd never drink again, but then I did. The pain of my last debauch would fade as the days passed until I forgot how much it hurt. I've also known cats that came to—cuffed to a hospital bed—told they were murderers when they awoke—fucking family killers, dream shatterers, just by getting behind the fucking wheel. Look, I know I'm a selfish fuck— I'd do anything to keep myself alive, but this time it's too much. I killed that girl and there ain't no good reason to keep me around.

I gathered Frank's canned goods and set them by the door. I packed up a few of his toys in a plastic bag and placed them by the chow. Frank's favorite—a fake fur mouse, I left on the floor.

I hate that fucking thing—it's horrifying. I can't tell you how many times I stomped on it—trying to kill it.

With the apartment in a state of order, I took a shower, and then with a sense of finality, put on a fresh pair of socks and my pajamas.

Do you ever get like that, when you know you're leaving? This is the last time I'll ever turn off this light or shut this door or water that plant. I'll never see my house again or lay on this bed. It's a long succession of good-byes.

I retrieved the gun from the closet and loaded it—walked to the living room with my fresh bottle of vodka—the gun and the bottle I placed on the desk.

My father suffered from black-outs—or maybe I should say, I suffered from his black-outs. At times I would plead for him to stop hitting me, but it fell on deaf ears—no, not deaf—he heard me and he answered in his fashion, but when drunk, I don't think he saw me as real. It was as if he was beating another boy. And when he was sober—even though my face showed signs of his abuse, there would be no admittance of his actions—and no remorse. I fucking hated him, and for me to remain here, knowing that I've now done worse than that piece of shit could ever aspire to, would be akin to cosigning his behavior—becoming him.

I unscrewed the cap from the bottle and took a drink. I wondered where Frank was and if he would be fine without me.

Fucking cats—as long as they're fed, eh?

A knock fell light upon the front door, and then louder it became as I stirred from my musing. A shadowy figure faded beyond the frosted glass—Matsudo.

"Are you hungry, Arthur? I have extra." The old man held up a brown paper bag, neatly rolled on top.

"No. Thank you. I don't care for Japanese food."

Matsudo shook his head. "You're a fucking racist."

"What?"

"It's a sandwich, you asshole—pastrami with a dill pickle and a side of thousand."

"I'm sorry—I thought it was—"

"I know what you thought"—Matsudo handed me the bag—"there's a fortune cookie in there too."

"A fortune cookie? That's Chinese."

The old man turned away—"On my mother's side."

CHAPTER ELEVEN—ROAD KILL

I woke early from a night bereft of dreams—Frank was curled at my feet. I cleaned myself up, fed the grey, and got dressed. My pajamas I tossed in the kitchen trash and I tidied what small mess I'd made in the house. I put Frank's food in a cardboard box and set the litter tray beside it. I called Burroughs.

"Hello?"

"Hey, it's me, Arthur"—there was a long period of silence, but no sign of disconnection—"Tom? I need to speak with you."

"What would you like to talk about? Do you know where Abigail Dupree is?"

"No. Why would I?"

"Arthur, if you're unwilling to be honest, I don't see what good this conversation does."

"I am being honest, but I don't wanna talk about her—it's something else."

"Do you know where she is?"

"No. I told you. No."

"Arthur, I saw you yesterday—you drove by her car."

"I know I did—I looked right at you. I would've stopped, but that morning…you know—you were kinda pissed at me."

"How did you know her car was there—that wasn't announced?"

"Lemke told me—when I was at the station. They wanted to talk to me about this thing—the thing I need to speak with you about—that's when I heard her car was there. Fuck. I'm not lying. I wish I did know where she was."

"Does John know where she is?"

"John?"

"Hawthorne," said Burroughs, "does he know where she is?"

"What the fuck? How would I know what he knows?"

"Arthur."

"Arthur, what? Fuck, Tom—you know me."

"Yes, I do. I know you as an irresponsible, violent alcoholic—that at one time I had hopes for. If you have information about Abigail, please tell me."

"I don't know a fucking thing about Abigail! I think I killed someone. Please—come on, man. I got no one else to talk to."

Again, an extended silence hung across the line—"I can meet you at the Green at 2pm…and son, you need to come straight."

"The Green? Why, the Green? There's too many fucking people there."

"Arthur, if you think I'm going to meet you in some private place, you're mistaken; and if you have killed someone, I'd recommend speaking to the police—or an attorney, instead."

"Okay. Fuck—I get it. I'll be there."

Burroughs was scared but…why? I've never harmed him. He can't possibly know what I've done—and the Green, fuck, the Green is hideous—a tourist park anchored in the center by a large, sculptured fountain of Medusa. I dig the monster, but she's surrounded by wannabe hip bistros and highbrow art vendors—a real jerk-off show.

I carried the box of cat food and Frank's other essentials downstairs and set them at Matsudo's door. I returned to my apartment—hesitated before placing Frank's life-like mouse in my pocket, and then I picked up the grey without making eye contact. I carried him downstairs. Matsudo was waiting.

"There he is"—the old man took Frank—"That's a lot of food. How much does a cat eat in a day?"

"One can, but you can sprinkle some of that other stuff on it—he likes that."

"One can?"—Matsudo eye counted the box—"How long will you be gone?"

"Fuck—not long, I just brought it all down because I'm fucking like that—I don't know, not long at all"—I reached into my pocket and fished out that nightmare of a mouse—Frank, in Matsudo's arms, pawed at the prize—"This thing's a fucking mind-fuck—terrifies me, but as you can see, the little fucker loves it"—I touched my boy's paw—"I appreciate you doing this, Mr. M—he's a real good little man."

I turned away.

I had plenty of time before I was to meet Burroughs so I took the long way to the coffee shop. I rode past the Singing Bridge and followed the Old Pier loop. The air tasted like home, and a sense of nostalgia saddened me. I wondered if anyone would miss me. I parked my bike out front and stepped through the door.

Jenny's bright pink hair was now blue. I figured the bands on her braces—like Matsudo said, had been changed to match.

If she was surprised to see me, it didn't register on her face—if anything, her look was one of disdain. We were alone. The burnt bitter coffee bean air was stifling.

"Hi, Daddy."

"Don't give me that fucking daddy shit—where's Heavy? Did he put you up to this?"

"Would you like a latte or a nice pumpkin spice?" She grabbed a cup from the counter.

"I wanna know what you gotta do with those fucking photos?"

"Blah-blah-blah—you're a fucking drunk."

"Hey, bitch, *you know* what I'm capable of!"

"You? You're not capable of anything, Mr. Limp-Dick. You should be worried about me."

"You—you're out of your fucking mind"—I advanced on the girl—furious—"I'm gonna give you a taste of what I gave her."

"Oh, a real tough guy, huh? How about this, Daddy"—she ripped her shirt—her left breast exposed—a small gold nipple ring flashed in the shop's dim light—"I called the cops when I saw you pull up. I told them that you'd threatened to rape me"—she tore open her button jean shorts, mussed her hair, and with the back of her hand smeared her lip gloss across her face—"Why don't you start beating me, Daddy, and I'll start crying?"

"I'm gonna fucking do you, bitch!"

The tingling bell on the coffee shop door signaled the arrival of a customer—two denim wearing, tattooed, biker wannabes seeking a mid-morning cup of chai tea.

"Help me!" Her high drama hysterics were perfectly staged—"He's hurting me!"

The men came towards me, and I towards them. The first silicone greaser dropped to his knees as I fired an I-don't-give-a-fuck-anymore kick to his balls; the second hippie went down following a straight shot to the bridge of his nose—his man bun hung in place as his body cascaded to the floor. The bikers' perfectly trimmed beard heroics were no match for my anger. I broke a chair and used one of its wooden legs as a club—Alternately, I beat the men until they cowered broken and spent. I discarded the wooden-chair leg and turned my attention to Jenny, but she was gone. The backdoor of the shop was open wide—the screen door bounced against the frame. Without hurry I left. The two greasy Good Samaritans moaning and sobbing in my wake.

On better days I might'a been concerned about another assault charge, but to be honest, they're not gonna have a chance to prosecute—and fuck those tattooed bitches anyway—if you're gonna pose, you better punch. I ain't gonna get too busted up about a couple of beaten down lames with stick-n-poke paintjobs.

I parked my bike behind one of the bistros and cut through a small working alleyway to the park. I clutched the envelope in my hand. Burroughs was already there—the old man looked as if he'd been cut from an old movie and spliced into his seat beneath a large white and gold umbrella. I wished that the beauty of the moment had fallen in a lighter time. I sat across from him.

"Fuck. I don't know where to start."

"Why don't you start with the police station? Why were you there?"

"They wanted to speak to me about a murder that I thought I didn't commit."

"Arthur, that doesn't make any sense. You thought you didn't kill someone?"

"I guess I did it, but I don't remember"—I put the envelope on the table—"I blacked-out."

"What's this?"

"It's photos."

Burroughs pulled the envelope across the table. "I'd laugh if I didn't think this was as serious as it is."

"What do you mean?"

He produced an almost identical envelope. "It's a photograph."

I reached for the package, but Burroughs held it back—
"Arthur, I want to believe you."

"I want you to," I replied, "I'm trying to tell you the truth."

"Okay, then, I'll show you what I have after you answer a question."

"I already told you, Tom. I don't know where the fuck she is."

"I want you to tell me about John Hawthorne."

"What the fuck is it with you and that fucking guy? I don't know him. I've never even seen him. Abigail mentioned him a few times—that's what she came to me for—you fucking sent her to me! He's extorting her. She needed help. Fuck that asshole!"

"You've never met him?"

"No. What the fuck? No!"

Burroughs pulled out the photograph. He placed it on the table as he stared into my eyes. He pointed to one of the two men in the picture—"Arthur, do you know who this is?"

"Yeah, it's me."

"And this man?"

"No, I never—I mean, I don't know when that picture was taken, but…"

"It was taken last week in the shop district. The man that you're speaking to is John Hawthorne. I had him followed."

I began to cry. "Fuck. I don't know what's wrong with me. I don't know any of this. I don't remember any of it. I'm at home. I'm always at home. I don't go anywhere. I don't know him."

"Arthur, is Abigail okay?"

"Fuck! I don't know. She left my house. I heard a car. I don't know."

"Arthur, did you hurt her?"

"No"—I picked up my envelope—"this is that thing. I don't remember it. I need help"—I handed the envelope to Burroughs—"look at it."

It remained unopened.

"Would you like me to take you?" said Burroughs.

"Take me where?

"To get help, Arthur. I think you need that."

"You mean jail, the fucking asylum? I can't do that. I won't."

I stood up—a quick panic attack reaction, and then, from the corner of my eye, I saw Roberts standing under an awning—Lemke and a uniformed officer were waiting near the restrooms. I calmly returned to my seat and spoke quietly to Burroughs.

"Tom, if I was the animal that you seem to think I am, at this moment, you would be getting thrashed within an inch of your life for your betrayal. I don't know what I've done. I don't feel capable of those things, but I can't deny what I've seen. I'm leaving, and if you do anything to alert those officers, I'll know that you never cared for me."

"Arthur, please, you need help."

I put my hand on Burroughs' shoulder. The old man tightened beneath my touch—"I'm leaving."

I turned and ran.

The Green was crowded for a weekday, but the oblivious tourists aided in my escape. I elbowed an old woman in the back as I cut between her and a small child. She went down hard. Her body, and the ensuing commotion, hindered my pursuers. I ran past the fountain and bulled through a habit of nuns before I turned into the small alleyway. There were large metal baking racks in the thoroughfare—I pulled them down behind me. I had my key in hand as I jumped on my bike. It was gonna be close. The cycle fired and I kicked it into gear. A hand grabbed the chrome bar of my seat, trying to impede my escape, but I stayed on the throttle—Fucking, Roberts, man. I grabbed his arm before he could disengage from the bar. I redlined the fuck out of the bike, but there was no way I was letting that asshole go. He lost his footing in the gutter and I drug him into traffic. I released him in front of a moving car—the following screeching tires and thump promised my deposit was well timed. I tore through the gears and lit out for the harbor.

I knew my pad would be cool for an hour or so—it would take the cops a while to regroup, and I was probably safe doing a quick in and out before I split town. Frank was fine with Matsudo. They wouldn't hassle the old man—and I didn't give a shit about my things—for all I cared, they could fucking burn 'em, but there was something I did need and it was worth the risk.

I pulled in front of the building and ran up the stairs. There was another envelope on my porch, but I stepped over it as I entered my place. The apartment was as I left it, everything in order, but the space felt uninhabited—empty without the presence of Frank. I grabbed my gun and the box of ammunition—shut the door without locking it, picked up the envelope, and ran past a worried Matsudo. Whatever the old man said, as I left, was unintelligible—*He was no more alive to me than I was.*

I figured I could shoot up the Coast Road and lay low near the stockyards without any hassle. Ultimately, I knew where I was going—it wasn't far, but I had to make sure I'd get there.

I pulled into the Sundowner motel.

I was not in the headspace to be amused, but the name was ironic; Drunks, drug addicts, hookers, and tramps, these are the inhabitants of the stockyards, a class of people that don't sleep at night. The Daylighter motel would'a been more apropos.

The desk clerk's one remaining strand of hair was dripping grease onto his thick pop bottle glasses. His teeth hadn't seen a brushing in years. I stood back.

"I need a room."

"We're twenty an hour."

"Are you fucking kidding me? I'm not dropping one-sixty on this shithole."

"One-sixty? How many are you?"

"It's me—just me, one night."

"We only have thirteen rooms."

"Thirteen rooms—what the fuck are you talking about?"

"I thought there were more of you."

I dropped a hundred-dollar bill on the counter—"Just give me a fucking key."

The clerk slid a small registration card and a pen toward me—"You gotta fill this out."

"Look, you fucking retard. You can write anything you want on that thing, but if you don't give me a key in two-fucking-seconds I'm gonna put that fucking pen in your throat."

Dull—he smiled, unconcerned.

"Hello?"—I tapped the side of his head—"Give-me-a-fucking-key, bud."

"Yes, sir," the man handed me a key.

He reached for the hundred. I beat him to it and put it back in my wallet—"You'll get that when I leave"—I flipped the key in my hand—"and if I get bugs from…uh…number seven, I'm gonna feed 'em to you."

"There's no bugs here—we spray"—he pushed a small pile of grey linen across the counter—"you need your sheets."

"Nah, I'm good."

I put the gun and the envelope in a dresser drawer, and then I parked my bike in the alley behind the room.

If the police do a drive-by, they won't see my ride. And the clerk surely has nothing to give 'em—that poor fuck was probably hired for the discretion his low I.Q. provides—like a fucking, child man. I almost feel bad for hassling him.

I walked to the corner liquor store unaccosted by the sidewalk dregs that made those streets their home.

I'm not sure why some people got victim written across their backs, and why others—without a visible hint of threat, portray predator. I was in no mood to be bothered, and being as I was already deep in it, I'd just as soon shoot you as tell you to fuck off— maybe those sidewalk curs caught that drift...

I went inside the market and asked for a fifth of vodka and a can of tuna before I realized that Frank was no longer mine—*I would've cried again, but I'd reached my limit of tears.*

The clerk set the bottle on the counter—"$10.50."

"Can I get a case of that?"

"Shit"—the clerk made a quick shelf check—"I don't think we got it."

"Well, what do you got there?"

"I've got six bottles left"—he reached up and hoisted a more expensive brand—"but I got this too, so yeah, I could do a case."

"Nah—fuck that noise, man"—I pulled out my wallet—"put that shit back. Give me those six bottles there and this one here— and a box, you got that, yeah?"

"Sure thing, bud."

I paid for the booze and walked out.

On the way back to the motel, I handed out the extra fifths— an early wet Christmas for a few lucky fucks.

For a moment I felt connected—as if I belonged—giving. Yeah, the booze was considered a vice of man, but at least we were all in it together. The feeling was short lived.

When I got to my room, I took off my shoes and lay down on the bare, piss stained mattress.

If I planned on living longer, I would surely get crabs, but even rats won't stay on a sinking ship.

Passively suicidal, I licked one of the uncovered pillows, and then I opened the Popov and tossed the cap over my shoulder— "You don't need the cap once the bottle is open; that's for transportation…ah…fuck it"—I stuck the bottle in my mouth and tilted my head back. The immoral clear liquid chanted, "Good, good, good," as it marched down my throat.

CHAPTER TWELVE—CHECKING OUT

How do you not feel remorse? I knew, as he sat across the table from me, that my bruised lips and my swollen eyes returned his gaze. And sometimes that was all I had—that no matter what he'd done to me, I could always look him in the eyes.

I remember the first time I thought of killing him. He'd left his gun on the counter; I picked it up and walked into his bedroom. He was asleep—lying face-up on the on the bed—dressed in a pair of plaid Sansabelt slacks and a polyester shirt peppered with cigarette burns. The gun felt good in my hand, and I knew it was loaded—'It's no good if it isn't.' And as I stood over him, I felt nothing, not even hate. I listened to his breath—ragged, uneven—at times he stopped breathing altogether, and then he'd gasp and rattle on. I knew it'd take nothing to do it, but instead, I put the gun on the nightstand beside his bed—hoping that in the morning, the doubt of whether or not he left it there would be upon him. I wanted him to think, that maybe, I had held his life in my hands, and I had spared him.

The toilet seat wobbled beneath my ass. I held my cock down as I urinated. With the door shut, I noticed a large hole drilled through the stucco and a light trail of blood sprayed up the wall.

Fucking cocksuckers and junkies, getting it on for twenty bucks an hour.

I washed up and made myself a hotel coffee in a clear plastic cup. I opened the drawer and pulled out the envelope and the gun—set them on the table—*I did my best to postpone my outcome, but I knew where I was heading.*

I walked up to the office and rang the counter bell. The girl that came from the back looked as if she'd just crawled out of bed—but even so, she was vibrant and attractive.

"Can I help you?"

"Yeah, I was wondering if you had the time, and when checkout is."

"It's noon o'clock, Baby—check out was an hour ago. What room you in?"

"Seven."

She pulled a registration card from a green plastic box on the counter. She read it and laughed. "Is that going to be cash or charge, Mr. Hole?"

"Huh?"

"I said, cash or charge."

"I heard that—what'd you call me?"

"Mr. Hole. That's how you signed in—A. Hole. Is there a problem?"

"No—that fucking asshole. That's alright—how much?"

"Well, you didn't take the sheets, so let's call it forty"—She put her hand on mine—"You all right, Honey?"

I pulled away—"Don't do that."

"Baby, I didn't mean anything by it."

"I didn't think you did. You just don't know any better"—I set a hundred on the counter and went back to my room.

I brewed another cup of coffee, and then I sat at the table. I opened the new envelope—my fears confirmed. It was a photo of Abigail. She was naked—tied to a chair, her head had been shaved, and it looked as if she'd been beaten. A note—written in black pen on clean white paper accompanied the photograph. It read:

I think the one of you holding her severed head is better, but she does look awfully cute here. Enjoy!

I put the note and the photo back in the envelope. As the thought of 'soon to be nothing' filled my body, I calmly—and without emotion, knew what to do. I washed my face, left the key on the dresser, and walked out the door. As I rounded the corner of the building, I came upon a tramp tampering with my bike.

"Walk away," I said.

"Fuck, dude, I was just looking at it."

"Walk away."

"You don't need to be a fucking bitch, man."

Ignoring him, I unlocked the saddlebag, and then I visibly placed the envelope and the gun inside. The tramp hustled off. I fired up the bike and took off for the cliffs. I had a half tank of gas—more than enough.

It was time to cash it in—but I wouldn't be putting a bullet in my mouth like my old man. My plan was to bust ass down the Monastery drive, crash through the guardrail, and sail onto the rocks below. There was honor in my decision. I wasn't a coward unable to face my weakness—I know what I fucking did. I was judge and jury, and now I was condemned—my death would be penance, not escape. The gun, I'm taking with me—a symbol of the honor that my father should've had.

I turned onto the Monastery drive, and after fifty yards or so, I cranked a U-turn. I had a slight James Dean feeling as I zipped up my leather and pulled down my goggles.

I wondered how my grandmother would feel about my choice, and instantly I knew her thoughts, "You're not God, Arthur. No man is. You can't see the whole truth."

I kicked the bike into gear and let it fly.

The difficulty in suicide is the argument before the decision—the 'should I' or 'shouldn't I.' After the decision is made, you either go back to your misery or you float toward your imminent demise. I was free as I sped toward the cliff.

For a moment I wondered if I should close my eyes or leave them open, then suddenly a blue flash appeared before me. I squeezed the front brake as I stomped on the rear pedal. The bike went into a slide. In what felt like slow motion, I bounced off the front fender of a blue '40 Ford and ricocheted into the bushes that lined the drive. The bike came to rest beneath a thick canopy of redwoods. I was dazed—lumped up, bleeding from a cut on my leg, but I was still alive. I stumbled my way up the embankment and stared into Burroughs' eyes.

"Motherfucker! I'm trying to kill myself, you reckless piece of shit."

CHAPTER THIRTEEN—THE GUESTS

"Jesus, Tom. What the fuck are you doing?"

"I'm trying to stop you—oh, God, look at my fucking car—God damn it, Arthur!"

"Your car? Look at my fucking bike!"

I climbed back into the bushes and attempted to retrieve my ride. The brambles and piles of leaves had softened the crash, but it was gonna be hell to fish out.

"Leave it"—the old man held out his hand—"come up here."

I pulled a thorny branch from my arm as I stepped onto the road—"What are you saving me for, so I can go to jail? Why don't you get the fuck out of the way so I can finish this?"

"Arthur, please—give me a moment—just one, fucking, minute."

Burroughs opened the driver's door of his Ford and retrieved the photos that I'd left at the Green. He handed me one—"Look at this."

"I don't wanna see those again. Fuck, man, what are you trying to do?"

"Arthur, look at it. Look at your face."

"I've seen it."

"Look at it!"

I looked at the photo—smiling, choking Nikki.

"Yeah, okay. I'm a real piece of shit—I get it."

"No!"—Burroughs pointed to the photograph—his finger below my left eye—"Look here."

"I can't fucking see it! I need glasses; I was gonna get some, but then I got all held up with this tax shit, and then Frank was going through some kind of a stretch, so I uh—"

"Look!"—Burroughs took off his glasses and used them as a magnifying lens—"No scar. There's no scar over your eye. That isn't you."

"What?"

"Look at your eye, you fucking nitwit!"

I bent down and stared through Burroughs' glasses —the scar wasn't there—"What the fuck? Did they alter it?"

"Yeah, that's what they did; they wanted you to look prettier, so they doctored the photo—come on, son. Arthur, I don't know what's going on here, but I don't think you killed her"—Burroughs put the photograph back in the envelope—"Now help me get my car out of the road—God damn it."

From the inside of his Ford, the damage wasn't noticeable.

"I'm sorry, Arthur. I should have believed you."

"Fuck"—I stared at the ocean—"I could'a been dead."

"You would have—if I hadn't stopped you"—his hands squeezed the steering wheel—"And Abigail—any contact with her? After seeing those photos, I fear the worst."

"I think she's gone—they said I killed her."

Burroughs was silent for a moment. "I think you should leave the bike here."

"In the bushes? Are you fucking kidding me?"

"They're looking for you. You can't ride that around—it's too conspicuous. I've got a car cover in my trunk—you can hide it. I don't think any of the brothers are going to walk down here. We could tell Father Tom that it's there, but if the police come looking for you, I don't think he'd stay silent."

I recalled my dealings with the old priest—"Nah—he'd probably be happier if you hadn't stopped me."

I grabbed the cover from Burroughs' trunk, returned to my bike, removed what I needed, and then I laid the machine on its side, draped it, and covered it with branches and leaves. It was invisible from the road. I returned to the car with the envelope, ammunition, and the gun—"I need to get my head straight."

Burroughs smiled. "Would you like me to hit you with something?"

"Ah, a return to the kindly father figure"—I squeezed the old man's shoulder—"thanks, Tom."

"The pleasure was all mine, Arthur—and as incorrigible as you are, you have been like a son to me. But right now, I'm aiding a fugitive, and as much as I'd like to sit here and revel in your continued existence, we have no idea what's going on—or who's against us. We need to find a place to lay up and work things out."

I remembered a soft hand and a recent cup of shitty coffee—"I think I've got an idea—I know a place in the Yards."

Burroughs drove like an old man—he gave it a little gas, and then he let off, and then he gave it a little more.

"You're driving me crazy with that fucking gas thing. Can't you just hold your foot steady?"

"Excuse me?"

"You're jerking my head all over the fucking place—I'm fucking injured, man."

"It's not me"—his foot moved up and down on the pedal—"it's the car—she's temperamental."

I'd worry that we're gonna be stopped for driving under the influence—the way he's jerking around, but if an officer pulled alongside, he'd see the old man at the wheel and chalk the uneven driving up to old age—shit, that's an excellent idea: drunk drivers should carry old man masks in their car, it'd cut down on arrests.

"Hey! What are you doing? You missed the cut off."

"No, I didn't. We've got to lose this car and get you some wheels."

We got off the highway and parked across the street from a car rental agency—"The One That Gets You There." The lot was full.

There was a late model black Maserati prominently displayed—"Get that fucking thing—the black one."

"That's ridiculous—I'm not getting that. Do you even have a license?"

"To drive?"

"Yes, a license to drive."

"Nope."

"What?"

"No. I don't got a license. I ride dirty"—It felt good to be alive.

"You're riding like an idiot—grow up." Burroughs shook his head as he walked away.

After about twenty minutes, and a whole lot of fiddling with the radio, Burroughs pulled up in a light blue minivan—tan interior.

"Are you fucking kidding me, Tom? Where's that Mausey?"

"It's on the lot. Get in—you're driving."

"I'm not driving that fucking thing."

"Arthur—focus, man, we're in a situation here. I need you to follow me."

"Let me drive your car."

"No"—Burroughs tossed me the minivan keys—"I think you've done enough damage to my car."

I got behind the wheel of the minivan. I adjusted the seat and checked my look in the mirror.

I was looking pretty good—what with trying to kill myself, and all. Yeah, I still had a couple of burrs in my hair, but I'd like to see you after a roll in a ditch—"To the motel?"

"No, my car would stand out in the Yards. No one knows I'm with you or assisting your disappearance, but we don't need anyone looking into why my car is parked at a cheap motel—I have a reputation to keep."

"Ha! Tom Burroughs—stodgy old prick, caught banging hookers and smoking cocaine at the Stockyard."

"Arthur."

"All right—just making light."

"Too much light—you're still in a predicament here. Follow me home, follow the rules—safe, simple, cautious driving. You don't want to get stopped."

"Okay, I'll follow the rules, but you keep the pedal down and smooth, right?"

"Screw you, Arthur."

Burroughs lived on the Hill—a real snobby ass enclave of left-wing crusaders. Don't get me wrong—I'm all for most of their causes; people should be treated like people—no matter what color or kind of people they are—and who they wanna fuck, suck, marry, or abort is their business. The environment definitely needs to be looked after, and it's imperative to think globally. But I'm not a big fan of some of their programs for the criminal offenders—you know—giving 'em all sorts of rights and shit, when they really just need a solid ass beating. Sometimes people are scum and they deserve to be treated as such—too many fucking lawsuits these days. I should be able to punch a motherfucker in the mouth, if he, she, or they are disrespecting; and the police should have that right too—although, if the police disrespect, well, then we should also have the right to slap 'em like a fucking sissy right in the kisser—or...drag 'em in front of a car, as the case may be.

I followed the rules, and Burroughs ignored my advice—the Ford lurched through traffic, as the old man catered to its "temperament." My frustration grew as we drove, but other than my discomfort, the ride to the Hill was uneventful.

When we arrived there was a police cruiser parked in front of Burroughs' place, so Burroughs had no choice but to pull into the driveway. I turned my face as I passed and drove on to an upscale grocery on the corner. I made sure the van was visible from the street, and then I went in for a cup of coffee. Six dollars later, I was back in the vehicle with a hot fresh cup of the expensive bitter black.

It was good, but it sure as fuck wasn't five dollars better than the Swill's brew—although you don't get a twice-fucked waitress sticking her dirty finger in it, so I guess that's a plus. I miss Frank, but now at least I might have a chance to see him again. Burroughs' discovery gave me hope—although with Abigail probably dead, the police still after me for who knows what besides murder, and my present inability to return home—I don't expect it to be anytime soon.

I faced the rearview mirror, and spoke to my reflection—"You're not sore at me for trying to do you in, are you? You know…at the time you deserved it. I thought you were a killer. I'm proud of you for going through with it though—you're an honorable motherfucker, that's for sure—and handsome too." I winked at myself.

The passenger door opened, and Burroughs slid in—"Are you doing your affirmations, Arthur?"

"Ha, you fucker. What's up down there?"

"It was your boy, Lemke—doing, of all things, a welfare check."

"Was Roberts with him?"

"No, Detective Roberts is in the hospital. He was hit by a car."

"Oh, shit, jeez, that's too bad."

Burroughs refused to swallow my feigned concern—"Have you eaten?"

I pointed at my cup of coffee.

"That's not food. Let's grab a couple of burgers. I'm starving."

"There's a chicken place by the motel."

"Arthur, you can get a chicken burger if you want, but I'm not eating down there. The last time I dined in the Yards, I lost twenty pounds."

"Well, then"—I poked Burroughs' ample stomach—"we should definitely do that."

He wasn't amused.

We sat in the minivan as we ate our meal in the Sundowner parking lot—a couple of burgers, fries, and I got a root beer.

"I don't think you should check in," said Burroughs.

"Are you fucking kidding me, at this place?"

I told him about the registration card and the rooms by the hour. He relaxed his pose.

"He doesn't sound mentally challenged to me, Arthur—or should I say, Mr. Hole?"

"Fuck you—that tard is running wild in there."

"I don't see him from here. It looks like a woman is at the desk."

"Pretty?"

"Is she pretty? How can I tell if she's…are you serious?"

I brushed back my hair and hopped out of the van—"I'm going in—come on."

She smiled as I opened the lobby door and walked up to the desk. Burroughs hung behind.

"You're back," she said. "You know when you left this morning, I didn't think I—or anyone else, would ever see you again —and especially with the esteemed Mr. Burroughs."

"You know each other?"

Burroughs stepped forward and removed his hat—"No. I don't believe we do."

She held out her hand—her fingers were long and shapely, her nails manicured and clean—on her neck, a praying hands tattoo.

"I'm Gracie, do you remember—Gracie—"

"—Abbot. Oh my God, you look just like your mother. I haven't seen you since you were a teen. Look at you"—Burroughs turned to me—"I worked with Gracie's mom—she was the best reporter our paper ever had"—he looked back to the girl—"I was sorry to hear of her passing. We had a lunch in her honor. She really was something."

"She thought the same of you"—Gracie smiled and the half-moon tattoo beneath her eye became full. She nodded toward me— "and now you're with this one."

"Yes," said Burroughs, "but don't let his rough edges fool you—inside, he's just as rotten."

The girl and Burroughs shared a laugh as I sat on the sidelines—"I guess I'm gonna have to remind you to focus—we are in the middle of a situation here."

"He's right"—Burroughs pulled out his wallet—"we need a room please—preferably quiet."

"You can have number twelve—it's on the end, by my place. I try to keep that section of the motel fairly private."

Burroughs fished out a large bill.

"No"—she waved him off—"there's no need for that. You're my guests, and…I think I still have Mr. Hole's registration card"—she laughed and pushed him two keys—"It's all yours."

The outside door opened, and the night clerk walked in.

"Hey, Gracie, I've got that window to fix in—" he grinned as his eyes met mine—"oh, excuse me."

"—Give me a second, Hank"—she turned to Burroughs—
"It was nice to see you…and him."

CHAPTER FOURTEEN—COLD FLESH

Number twelve had two full beds and a small sitting room. The beds came made with clean linens, and there was an absence of bathroom blood-trails and naughty boy gloryholes. Burroughs took a seat at the small table.

"This isn't that bad. The way you made it sound, I thought we'd be fighting off rat-sized bugs."

"Yeah, well, this isn't the room he gave me—I've probably got crabs."

"They probably assign room to renter—as a matter of fact, you do seem a touch dressed down for this chalet."

"Well maybe I should'a chatted up ol' Hank in there, and he would've taken good care of me like she did for you."

"Arthur, I've known her since she was a little girl—and I loved her mother—although little Gracie seems to have fallen on hard times...I heard she'd had some troubles."

Burroughs hung his hat on the mirror over the dresser.

"I don't know anything about her troubles, Mr. B, but as I see it, she isn't in hard times at all—if anything, she's coming up. She's got miles, sure, and her clothes—definitely second hand, but her eyes are clear—you don't get shine like that when you're down; that comes from life, man, not death—smell that paint, check those linens, they're not expensive, but they are new. I think she's stepping up—sticking the sleazy, fuck-by-the-hour, check-in trash in the old rooms, and shaping this place into a nice little motel. Did you see her tattoo—a pair of praying hands? Miss Gracie is probably sober—she looks it. I bet she's doing all right."

"You amaze me, Arthur; just when I think that you're beyond redemption, you open up that running hole of yours and out comes hope—and for her sake, I hope you're correct"—Burroughs walked to the window. He stared beyond the parking lot and into the past—"Her mother was beautiful; I remember the first day I saw her—her hair lying in light rainy-day wisps upon her face—her eyes, the color of a late fall leaf...she was exquisite...and so warm...I wish I wasn't so blind...so set in my ways..."

He drifted into silence, and I let him be. His depth of feeling—in regard to Gracie's mother was something I knew nothing about. Other than my grandmother, I'd never felt for a human the way I felt for Frank—the way I've heard others feel. Fuck that noise, man. People can't be trusted. You never know what they're thinking or what games they're playing, and then one day they just get up and split, or sure, maybe they stay, but their heart has gone to market. I'm not gonna put anything of myself in that— something that fragile. Frank, he barely changes—he's a safe bet, a sure thing—that little fucker is practically static; he and I live in a world set apart from betrayal—protect him from harm, feed him, love him—he'll never leave me.

Burroughs grabbed a pad of paper and a pen from a small drawer in the desk. "Did you catch the name? The Sundowner?"

"Huh?"

"The name of the motel, she does have a sense of humor— a young black girl owning property in an old sundown town."

"Yeah, well, before you get all settled in, and feeling too sundowny, I'm gonna step out for a minute. I gotta get something to wash down that fucking burger."

"I don't think you should be wandering around. The police are looking for you—if you really need something, I'll go."

"You're out of your fucking mind, Chief—no offense, but your old ass would get robbed out there—and I doubt the police are cruising Jr.'s Market—you better sit tight."

I excused myself to the liquor store.

When I returned, Burroughs took a hard look at the fifth in my hand—"I'm not drinking," he said.

"I didn't think you were. Here"—I tossed him a chocolate bar—"candy is dandy."

"And liquor is quicker—come on, Arthur, I need your wits about you."

I pulled up a chair and faced the old man—"And this is gonna float those wits right on up to the surface"—I took a grateful drink—"What do you got, Pops?"

"I've got this"—Burroughs had the photos, pen, and paper arranged on the desk—"we need to put it down on paper to see if anything lines up—when it comes right down to it, neither one of us knows what the hell is going on"—he pulled the pad before him—"now, tell me your side—all of it—and I'm assuming that you were sleeping with Abigail, so don't start out by lying."

"I wasn't…"—the old man looked into my eyes and held his gaze—"okay, it was like twice—but that's not really 'sleeping with;' that's just getting to know each other—expanding trust with the client—you know?"

"Arthur, you are so full of shit. Come on"—my bottle was quickly heading toward half-empty—"while you still can."

I was surprisingly honest. It's not that I don't have a good relationship with the truth—I do, but sometimes the truth needs a little something extra to help it along.

I began at the black sedan, and I walked Burroughs through to my attempted demise. As I spoke, he caught my story in old newspaper shorthand.

"...And I would'a done it, if I hadn't have crashed into you."

"Hmmm, that's quite a tale, Arthur. So, you saw the sedan before Abigail had arrived—and you have the key, but she never gave you the number?"

"She said she didn't know it. I figured you knew what it was."

"I didn't know there was a locker—let alone a key. And I'm wondering about that car that followed you. You couldn't make it?"

"No. the lights were on me."

Burroughs sat quietly for a moment, and then he launched into a flurry of writing as I saw to my bottle. After a few moments, the old man put the pen down and set the papers side by side.

I glanced at his work—"I may be a little fucked-up, but even without the buzz on, I couldn't read that."

Burroughs laughed. "No one can"—he walked over to the desk and returned with a clear plastic wrapped motel cup. He removed the thin sheathing and set the vessel before me—"two fingers, please—if there's any left."

"We can always get another"—I poured slightly short of the requested amount.

Burroughs continued. "When Abigail came to me, I knew she was being dishonest—there was no cheating husband or needy friend—it wasn't her style. I didn't know what was happening, but I knew that whatever it was, it needed discretion, so I thought of you. I warned her that you could be a bit of a ...wildcard—"

"Yeah, thanks for that."

"—But I also said that you could be trusted. Although, I had no idea to where her story was leading. Grayson, on the other hand, was a different issue. I liked him; he took chances—dug in hard, and he wasn't one to let up when things got rough. He called me one night and said he needed to meet with me. He seemed…I don't want to say scared, but he was adamant that it be soon. I told him that I could come immediately; we set a time and a place, but then he stood me up. My calls to him went unanswered—It was a few days later that he finally contacted me. He was very short—clipped, as if he was being pressed, he said, 'Get ahold of Abigail—Port Authority— she has it—'and then we were disconnected. Again, any attempt I made to reach him, came to naught; the next evening he supposedly took his own life."

"Supposedly? You don't believe it? Abigail didn't think he had it in him."

"No, I don't believe it—he wasn't the sort; I'm just telling you what I was told—the facts as they were. I contacted a photographer that Grayson often worked with—a freelancer, Jason Horn—trying to make a name for himself—an honest hustler, if you will. I acted as if I had an assignment for him—which in a way, I did. I had a feeling that if David was digging around—Horn was in on it. I was right. Horn said that David had him staking out a few places. He'd given him some names and a few faces to look for— one of them was your old friend, T. Terry. I asked if he had any idea what David was investigating—he said it sounded like a drug ring of some sort, but that Grayson had hinted at something more, something darker. I told him to stay on it and stay low. We met some time later—after I had sent Abigail to you, and he showed me what he had."

Burroughs pulled from his envelope a small collection of photographs.

"That's fucking Paul, man—the midget, Paul."

"Hang on a second. Let me lay these out"—Burroughs dealt out three photos—Paul, T. Terry, and John Hawthorne—"I'm sure you're familiar with this crew."

"Paul and Terry, yeah, but there's your man again—fucking Hawthorne."

"John."

"Yeah, whatever—so what's the link? How do I figure into this?"

"Here's how"—the old man dealt out another photo— *Hawthorne and 'the man who would be me' standing close in conversation*—"you could imagine how I felt when I saw this. I thought that I'd sent Abigail into the wolf's mouth—and then she went missing. I cursed myself for making the call that had set you free."

"Set me free?"

"Your recent arrest—Nikki Graves."

"Fuck—it was you?"

"I didn't think you were a killer, Arthur—hold on a minute, let me rephrase that, I didn't think that you were a killer of women— violent, yes, but you do have that streak of misogynistic chivalry. I still have acquaintances downtown, so when I heard you were in, I immediately got you out—before you could get yourself into trouble—although, from what I heard, you'd already done some damage."

"Yeah well, that fuck, Roberts, told me that he killed Frank, and he set me up for a beating, and then...uh...I did hold one thing back."

"Arthur, I told you that honesty was imperative."

"I drug Roberts in front of a car—there I said it—if he had tits, I wouldn't have done it though, right?"

Burroughs rolled his eyes and took a sip of his drink—"Let's just pretend you didn't tell me that."

"Tell you what?"

"Exactly"—the old man paused and wiped his handkerchief across his brow—*he wasn't sweating, it was more habit than need*— "The morning we met for breakfast, I wanted to hear what you knew—and I'm sorry for walking out on you, but when I saw your eyes, I knew that you knew about Grayson and Hawthorne."

"But I didn't."

"You knew the names, and I had the photo of who I thought was you—at the time that was everything I needed to know. I read too much into it. I guess I'm getting older—soft; I was worried about Abigail. I should have played it cooler, and in time, we would've fallen onto the same page."

"Do you think she's dead?"

"I hope not—the photo you have proves nothing. I'm thinking that if she was dead, they would've shown you—and look at this."

Burroughs pulled out the photo of Abigail and set it beside the shot of Nikki's torture.

"How can you look at that shit?"

"I remove emotion, Arthur—as you do, at times—it's not easy—it's professional."

I did my best to be cold—unfeeling, and when I crossed into the pain in Abi's eyes—I buried the hurt.

"These photos were shot in different rooms—different lighting. The shot of Abigail is of poor quality—rushed, amateurish in its lack of depth. This"—Burroughs touched the photo of Nikki—"is a professional shot."

"Paul. That has to be his connection to the crew, and if he's in, you can bet that fucker, Dick Heavy is with him."

"Dick Heavy?"

"I guess you don't watch much porn."

"No—I don't."

"That shot of Nikki looks like their work—although, I didn't figure 'em as accessories to murder."

"And you still can't—at least not yet." The old man put another shot of Abi on the table. I laughed.

"Really?"

"I'm sorry, but that little fucker in the saddle…"

He rolled past my immaturity. "Now this shot is the same as Nikki's—see the lighting, the room…"

"—And the look in Abigail's eyes."

"What?"

"She's participating. This is why I didn't believe her—I thought she was fucking with me. Does it look as if she's been drugged?"

"Not to me, but maybe she has been, and if so, could this be the same thing that you drank on the pier?"

"She said that Hawthorne had used it on her friend—it has to be."

"It doesn't have to be, but at this stage, it's likely. When I left the restaurant that morning, I cruised the waterfront. I was the one who found her car."

"Fuck—I'm surprised you didn't set the boys on me then."

"I did"—the old man looked away—"I told them that I thought you had something to do with it—thank God I didn't show them the photos after you made your escape, but I did set you up."

"You, fucking rat"—I drained my bottle.

"And if they would've grabbed you..."

"Yeah, I would've been hanging on a murder slash kidnapping rap—a straight up death sentence. But I still don't see how the fuck I got involved. Why the fuck are they pinning this on me?"

"On my end, it was a coincidence that brought you in, but it looks like you were wanted before I sent Abigail your way."

I held the empty fifth in my hand and wistfully remembered the bottle's opening—"I don't get it—Terry, Paul, and Hawthorne— the evil Arthur, what the fuck should we do?"

"If we were the police, we could start beating bushes by pulling them in and hoping that one of them breaks or turns—but I'm not sure what that would mean for Abigail. If you're asking me what I think, I'd say drugs, blackmail—your standard low-level criminal behavior—it's piddly shit, but then we have this other you—and murder and kidnaping...we need the connection that we can't see"—Burroughs wiped his brow again—"Let me look at the key."

"I don't got it."

"What?"

"Well, I've got it, but it's not here. It's at my house—stashed. To be honest, I wasn't thinking about it when I left, but I can't go back there now—my place is sure to be hot."

Burroughs closed his eyes for a moment.

"I'm tired"—the old man took off his shoes and laid down on the bed—"sometimes it's best to let your mind work as your body rests. I suggest you do the same."

"Tuck me in?" I said.

"Tuck yourself in, and I hope that you don't snore. I sleep light these days."

"And Abigail?"

"There's nothing that we can do tonight."

CHAPTER FIFTEEN—DIRTY SOCKS

The scent of morning coffee woke me.

Burroughs sat at the table in his t-shirt and underwear. His black socks were pulled up above his calves; his brown leather shoes were on and tied… He was hard at work, and from the look of it, had been so for some time.

"Are you fucking kidding me, Pops? Put some pants on. How long have you been up?"

"Arthur, what's your earliest memory of your childhood?"

"Jesus. I haven't even pissed yet—give me a minute, huh."

I staggered my way into the bathroom.

The lid of the toilet was down, so I pissed in the sink. I called to Burroughs through the open door—"Why is this lid down? What the fuck were you doing in here? Were you getting weird?" I turned on the water and talked over the competing stream—"I remember my mother ironing. I was too short to look over the ironing board, so I must'a been either four or five. Why?"

I walked out of the bathroom and coaxed a cup of coffee from the room's two-cup coffee maker—it groaned as if it were ill—"I can't drink this shit, man—it's fucking vile."

"Do you remember anything else from that moment—details?"

"Yeah, she was listening to a song as she worked—she was wearing green peg-leg pants, house slippers, and a white blouse—are you listening to me? I can't drink this shit"—I set my half-filled cup of cold, coffee impersonating liquid on the table—"Her hair was in curlers, and she seemed happy."

"That's a very vivid memory. Was there anyone else in the room?"

"Nah, not that I recall."

"Your father? Anyone?"

"No. I told you. That's it—and even that's in doubt. Sometimes I think I make this shit up. What are you thinking?"

Burroughs was musing over the photo of the man who looked like me and the man who was Hawthorne. "It's this…this other 'Arthur'—you have no known relations?"

"No. You know my story."

"You were taken from your father…"

"—His body…not him. I was taken from a hotel room in which his dead body lay. That piece of shit wouldn't'a let me go. He might'a beat my ass on the regular—called me the sore half of the split, but that motherfucker had his grip wrapped around me like a winning lottery ticket—for what, I don't know."

"And you're thirty-eight now? Your birthdate?"

"January eighth, I'll be thirty-nine. Why? Where are you going with this? There's no record of my birth."

"That they found no record of your birth, doesn't mean that there isn't one. Have you ever visited Child Services? I have. It's a miracle that they didn't lose you in transit. I doubt much effort was put into your case."

"They found my grandmother."

"That's a different story—not difficult at all, and even so, it took them what, six months to locate her?"

"Yeah, a year—six months—something like that, but who gives a fuck?"

"We do. I don't think Arthurs grow on trees—he had to come from somewhere."

"A distant relation perhaps—royalty from overseas"—I posed like a princess in front of the window—"maybe I'm a lord."

"More like the King of Fools, boy"—Burroughs laughed—"We've got some serious work ahead of us."

"Excellent"—I stretched and threw a pantomime punch—"I'm ready to start beating some bushes."

The old man stood up and looked at himself in the mirror—his eyes were still younger than the face that enclosed 'em—vigor, that's what they call it—life.

"I'm afraid to say this," said Burroughs, "but I think you might be right. We might need to startle some birds, and I'm thinking you should start here"—he put his finger on a photo—"T. Terry—stay away from Hawthorne for now and remember, you're not in control here. We don't know who is against us—and Arthur, don't forget"—he stifled a laugh—"you're a wanted man."

"What's so funny?"

"I was about to give you an ominous 'Trust No One,' and then I remembered that you already don't trust anyone…so…trust someone?"—As Burroughs said it, a light knock fell upon the door. He got to his feet and into his trousers.

"Relax, it's not the cops. They're not so polite."

Burroughs opened the door and a smile crossed his face—"Good morning."

I mussed my hair and exacted a cool casual pose. Gracie came into the room with a small tray of two large coffees and a couple of scones.

"I saw the light on and I figured you might like something."

She set the tray on the table—careful not to look at or disturb Burroughs' work. She picked up the cheap plastic cups and tossed them in the trash. Her eyes took a slow walk over me.

"I'm surprised you don't have little hearts on those—or maybe a unicorn."

Acting as tough as my bikini briefs allowed, I leaned like a gunfighter against the wall as I pulled my slacks on—"I got a pair that says, 'watch it,' but I left those at home."

"Ha! Well, you enjoy your little panty party and if you need another round, I'm in room thirteen."

She unexpectedly hugged Burroughs and walked toward the door.

"Gracie," said the old man "could we trouble you for another night? We appreciate your generosity but—"

"Mr. Burroughs…Tom. We've got plenty of room here, and to be honest, the thought of you staying comforts me—reminds me of my mother. If it'd make you feel better—and you'd like to toss a few bucks in, there's a place up front to donate to our local outreach"

"Coffees and such?" I asked.

"Yes—drunks do like their hot coffee—don't they?"

Burroughs laughed—"He sure does. I'd be glad to donate, and we appreciate the hospitality."

She closed the door behind her.

I stood before the mirror—"Do you think I'm a drunk?"

Burroughs choked on his coffee. He wiped his lips with his handkerchief—"Who are you asking?"

"I think, she thinks I'm a drunk. I've got Frank, a motorbike, a nice place to live—I'm a detective, not a drunk. Drunks are homeless and they're usually not mechanically mobile."

"Are you messing with me, Arthur?"

"No, I just…uh…wondered."

"Arthur, you had a grandmother that made sure that you'd be okay financially because she knew—and I hope this doesn't offend you, that without her endowment you'd be out on the streets. Yes, I think you're a drunk. Now can we lay out a plan?"

"Maybe I should become a monk? Leave it all behind—take Frank and move to the monastery—change my life."

"That sounds wonderful. I'm sure Fr. Tom would be thrilled"—Burroughs turned back to his work. "I think you should start, as I said—with T. Terry, but go easy—or as easy as possible—we don't want to create panic, but we do want movement. I've got a few things I need to see about—put brains to your brawn, so to speak—and we need that locker key. That car rental place opens at 9am, but I think you should take me to the airport. I'll pick up another car there, and then I'll go see Mr. Matsudo. We can rendezvous back here tonight."

I reached down and pulled off one of my socks. I handed it to Burroughs—"Will you give this to Frank?"

"Your dirty sock?"

"Yeah"—I smiled—"he loves 'em."

Burroughs put the sock in his pocket—"Yes, I'll give him your sock. Now get dressed and let's get moving"—he tossed me a scone—"and here, put something in your stomach—Brother Arthur."

It wasn't the bike, but the minivan's seats were soft—it handled well, and I enjoyed the radio—I just didn't wanna be seen in it—and not because I'm a fugitive. I dropped Burroughs at the airport, and then I drove toward The Nest.

This detective shit isn't what you think it is. There's no fucking Sherlock Holmes up in here, no Poirot, no Columbo bumbling about—these cops and private dicks aren't sitting around with a slide rule and a crystal ball making brilliant, rocket science, magic. They ask simple, down to earth questions—who's closest to the victim, who might profit from the crime, where's the victim been hanging his hat—a bunch of boring noise. They interview these cats and they match stories—looking for inconsistencies. As Burroughs said, 'they beat the bushes, and see who flies.'—In the old days, they used to beat the suspects and see who cries. Well, you can chalk me up as a nostalgic type—I open my gifts on Christmas Day—not

Christmas Eve, and I prefer a hard rocking punch in the mouth to get things rolling—people know you mean business when you loosen a tooth or two.

I stopped at a corner market for a coffee and a cherry Danish. I bought a cheap toothbrush and a small tube of Crest. On my way back to the van, I grabbed a newspaper and an expensive domestic cigar from a sidewalk stand—*I don't smoke trash*, and then I drove to the alley behind The Crow's Nest and set up shop. I ate the Danish, brushed my teeth—rinsing with a few sips of hot coffee, then I lit the cigar and opened the paper. Abigail's picture was on the front page. They announced her as missing. A reward was offered—they were seeking suspects.

I bet her father is going out of his fucking mind. If it were me—and I had his money, I'd have this whole fucking town on lockdown—and when the perpetrators were caught, those motherfuckers would never see a trial. I'd do 'em all. One of my therapists once told me that I got a strange sense of justice; it's based on my father and my resentment towards him—he'd never paid for what he'd done to me—at least not properly, so I'd transferred that onto those I thought had traversed proper judgment, and I took to it personally to mete out payment accordingly. Ha! I remember sliding forward on my chair, leaning toward her, and asking if she felt afraid—I was just fucking with her. "No," she said, "I don't feel afraid at all, I feel sorry for you."

I was glad I bought the paper—it was hours before T. Terry arrived. I'd just reclined my seat for a quick nap when I heard his Mustang pull into the alley—I remained low.

Terry parked his car, and then he walked to the backdoor. I climbed out of the van and stood quietly behind the club owner as he put his key into the lock.

"What's up, Terry."

As he turned, I punched him in the face—a hard connecting shot to his nose. Terry's head slammed into the door as he slid down upon his ass. The blood was instantaneous; the fear came secondary.

"Fuck, don't kill me"—he tried to slide backwards, but the door blocked his exit—"Arthur, please, man, don't fucking kill me!"

"Now why would I kill you?"—I grabbed his hair and pulled him to his feet—"Why don't you just open the fucking door and let us in?"

"Arthur please..."

"Don't 'please' me, bitch. Just do it."

Terry opened the door, and I kicked him in the back. He fell to the floor and crawled away from me. I followed him in.

"I've never been in the kitchen of this shithole—is this what goes on back here?"

He tried to get to his feet, but I kicked him into a cabinet. He scuttled on his ass into a corner as I grabbed a large knife from a rack on the wall.

"This here is bigger than I like, but I'm not gonna waste a bunch of time on you—making precision slits to gain micro bits of information. I'm gonna carve me a big 'ol fucking chunk—gut ya, so to speak. When this fucker goes in—it's going in once, and it's going in to stay."

"Fuck, man, I'm your friend—your fucking friend, Arthur."

"I don't like the foul language, Terrance. I don't think it's appropriate in times like these. What would you like to tell me?"

"About what? Fuck, man, come on."

I grabbed his leg and pulled off his shoe—*Nike*.

"Arthur, what are you doing?"

"I'm thinking about taking off a toe or two, but this uh, dull blade—you can't afford something better, something a touch sharper—maybe one of those Japanese knifes—those Ginsu—or whatever the fuck they call 'em? I don't think this edge is gonna go through your bones."

"Please, man. Don't hurt me. I have no idea—I didn't tell

anybody anything."

"Tell anybody? Tell anybody what? What would you tell someone? Did you say something that would make me wanna hurt you?"

"The thing, the other night, the girl, the kid, fuck, man, I've got your fucking back."

I stood up and set the knife on the grill. There was a hose coiled up on the floor—"My fucking back, huh?"—I uncoiled the line and threw an end over a large iron pipe that ran the length of the ceiling—"What's that look like when you've got somebody's back?"—I fashioned a quick noose.

"Arthur, what are you doing?"

"You've been depressed."

"No, I haven't"—Terry began to cry.

"You were lying to your friends, and you were being bad. You couldn't take it anymore."

"Please, Arthur, no."

You can only push a man so far—it's a real science, and I don't mind saying how good I am at it—you know, knowing how far you can take it. If you don't push 'em enough, they'll lie—hold out on you. If you push 'em too far, they'll break—retreat into a catatonic state, and you can't get shit out of 'em. I was in danger of losing Terry—and check it out, one punch was all it took—the rest was chatter, perceived threats between friends—he didn't have much of a constitution—fucking tattletale.

I pulled up a kitchen chair and sat next to my pal. I leaned over him—"I'd like to know about Paul. What do you know about him?"

"Paul? What Paul? Bartender Paul? What are you talking about?"

I grabbed the blade from the counter—"That's not the way I'd like this to go"— I touched the knife to T. Terry's cheek, slowly dragging the tip towards his neck—"When I say a name or ask about anything, I'd like you to just start talking—no questions. If I don't like where you're going, I'll stop you. Okay?"

Terry said nothing.

"Look, Terry, I understand you're probably upset with me—and I don't blame you, but wouldn't you like this to go better for you—a happy ending, so to speak?"

"Yes."

"Good. Now, I'd like to know about the midget, Paul. What can you tell me about him?"

I could see the terror in his eyes—the pupils dilating as he sought a pathway to not get hurt—and, I hate to admit it, but it was kinda turning me on.

"He's small and black, and the one time I bought him a drink, he got a lemonade and vodka which I thought was kinda faggy for someone like him—he tries to come off tough and...fuck, Arthur, I'm not sure what you're looking for...I'm trying—"

"Okay, okay, that's good—you're doing very well"—I touched the point of the blade to his forehead—"Now, this next bit might be a little harder, but I want you to do good, so I'm gonna help you. You see, what I've noticed is, that when you're telling the truth, you look up and to the left; right here"—I quick cut the top left corner of T. Terry's eye. He put his hands to his face and screamed. I gave him a little kick—"You better quit being a bitch, Terry. I'm trying to help you. You put your hands down now—come on...do it—put 'em down—do it."

Terry lowered his hands.

"Good. You see—that's how fucked up this knife is, it's dull—looks like it tore more than it cut—but okay, okay—we can get this. Now, you might not take me for someone who likes to read, but I do; I really enjoy it—mostly old science fiction, but sometimes I read books that are...well...nonfiction"—Terry touched his eye—"Am I boring you, Terry?"

"Arthur, I...don't, I—"

"—I mean…we could just get right to it, if you want—is that what you want?"—*He looked like a child holding back tears. I felt nothing. Well, not compassion for sure—and not elation, I guess I felt— unconcerned and slightly aroused. I go through most days feeling ill, as if I'm constantly dying—and I've been called a hypochondriac on a few occasions—I'm always contracting something. But being occupied, putting Terry to it, kinda took my mind off my ailments. I liked it*—"Anyway, as I was saying, sometimes I read books of an educational variety. And one day I was reading some CIA type literature—pertaining to interrogations— you know, something that I could use on the job, and they said that you could tell if a man's lying by the movement of his eyes. The crazy thing is, even if you decided to fuck me around—and I had to cut your eyes out—when I ask you a question, your muscles around the hole where your eyes once were, would still jerk toward the upper left, but only if you're telling the truth. So that's why I marked that spot—so I can see when you're being honest, and then I won't have to hurt you. Now, I'm gonna ask you a question, and I'm gonna watch your eyes—look right here—wait, hang on a minute, let me set this down"—I set the knife on the floor and held Terry's head between my hands—"Now look right at me—yes or no answer, do you know John Hawthorne?"

"Yes."

"Yay!"—I clapped like a child and giggled as Terry sobbed—"See, you did it. You never have to be cut again. Tell me what you know, and I'll watch your face. I don't wanna hurt you, buddy."

"He showed up a few weeks ago, wanted me to push a drug for him. He called it, Hypno—I'm not sure why. It was worthless. I couldn't have made anything from it—it wasn't recreational; it was the kind of thing a creep would lace a drink with. I took it myself one night—just to see what it would do, and I came to a few hours later, in the same place, with no memory of the past. I told him, no— I don't handle shit like that—no hard feelings, but it's not my thing.

He didn't seem too disappointed."

"Excellent. Is there anything else about Paul or Hawthorne or anything at all that you'd like to share with me?"

"No"—he squeezed his eyes shut and grimaced—"no, there's nothing. I can't believe you hurt me like this. I didn't do anything."

"Yeah, well, I've got issues—and innocence is all relative—we've all done something. Give me your car keys."

"My keys?"

"Terry?"

"Okay"—he unfastened a large ring of keys from a clip on his belt—"here—are you going to kill me now?"

"No. I'm driving a minivan and I don't like it. I'm gonna borrow your car for a bit, and you can drive mine. You've gotta be careful though—it's not in my name."

"But…"

"If anyone asks you, you got in a small fender bender—that explains the eye and the nose. Your car is at the shop, and you'll be good to go soon. Okay?"

He nodded.

"And I noticed that little fenced in room there—the booze storage place. Do one of these keys open that lock?"

"Yes."

"Which one is it?"—I held out the ring; Terry, with a bloody finger, touched a grey master lock key—"Thanks, buddy. I'd like to get a little something to go, and then I'm gonna hit the road"—I unlocked the gate and retrieved a fifth of vodka—*Smirnoff, slightly better name, same vodka taste.*

I took the car keys off the ring and handed the rest to Terry—"I don't need all these—you're gonna want 'em—and I'm sorry for calling your place a shithole—I like it here."

He said nothing.

"And about that minivan, it's not too showy, but I think you'll enjoy it. It's extremely comfortable—and it's got a nice little radio."

        I walked outside and fired up his Mustang.

        T.Terry picked up the phone.

CHAPTER SIXTEEN—MOMMY ISSUES

"James Ichabod Chance; Salem Oregon, address: 2600 Center St. NE, arrested for book-making."

"Ichabod? No wonder he was such an asshole—almost makes me forgive him"—I washed my hands—the knuckles on my right were cut—dried blood congealed—"Motherfucker probably had a string of arrests."

"No, surprisingly not as many as I thought, but Arthur—listen up, son, this was almost thirty-nine years ago. He lived in Salem when you were born—or should I say, when his boys were born."

"His boys?"

"Yes, you have a twin brother, and your father received—as you said, 'the sore half of the split.'"

"That's fucking ridiculous! And, what's his name, Unicorn Boy? Come on, Tom."

"Arthur, I'm telling you what I found—take it as you will, but this makes a hell of a lot more sense to me than some random look-a-like. You have a brother."

This time, as Burroughs said it, it was as if I'd returned to my youth—I could see my brother's face—my face. It was in the aftermath of an afternoon beating. I was trying to soothe him—holding the boy as he cried. The night that my father took me–the table for two, I was protecting him from our father's rage. I felt sick.

"How the fuck could I forget that?"

"I'm not a psychologist, Arthur, but you're not new to blacking out."

"Blacking out on booze, yeah, but I was a kid."

"You were a kid who was beaten, abused, neglected, and torn from his mother—do I need to go on?"

I splashed water on my face; it did little to hide my tears.

"And my mother—do you know where she is?"

"No idea. I have her maiden name, but nothing else—Elena Godfrey; she was only fifteen when you were born. She listed the same address as your father."

I moved about the room—randomly folding towels, wiping surfaces, and smoothing the covers of our beds—"In one day, you found me an underage mother and a delinquent brother—any name on this…evil Arthur?"

"James Francis Chance, born twenty-three minutes your junior."

"Francis, as in, Frank? Oh, fuck no."

"Look, Arthur, I get it—it's a lot to swallow—"

"—You don't get anything. I'm sitting in a fucking motel room, wanted for murder, and you tell me that my mother was an underage slut—"

Burroughs slapped my face.

Instinctively, I grabbed the old man's arm and forced him to his knees—"Don't you ever lay a fucking hand on me—I'll fucking kill you, man."

The room became silent but for my heavy breathing and the old man's pained gasps for air.

I released his arm and walked out.

The air outside was cold; the motel parking lot empty—save for two cars—T. Terry's Mustang and what appeared to be Burroughs' new rental—*looked like a fucking Civic or some shit. This is why old people shouldn't be out on their own—poor choices.* I stood outside the door and did my best to hold down the tears until I gave into the pain. I began to walk, and then a slight run, and then as I reached the highway, a full speed sprint. I ran on self-pity, and then on anger, and then on the feeling of remorse for the violence I'd just inflicted on Burroughs. I ran until the hurt of the evening left me, and when I could run no more, I stopped—miles away from the Sundowner—my bare feet blistered in my shoes.

I don't know what I'd been hoping for—this fantasy of a child with an absent parent—thinking that the missing unit is somehow perfect—existing in a world beyond and above my reality of life. So what, she was fucking him when she was fifteen, it doesn't make her bad—stupid, yeah—hooking up with that fucking prick, but not bad—not less. I wonder where her fucking parents were— who lets their kid get knocked up at that age? Oh well, c'est la vie— life is shit. I guess on the good side, she's only fifteen years older than me—that'd make her fifty-four or so. If she's still alive—and not a blown-out prostitute, drug addict, or a drunk; we might be able to have a nice little conversation one day. Maybe my new murderous brother will know where she is. I'll send her a Christmas card.

As I turned back toward the motel, I had a moment of cautious sanity; I crossed the street so my face wouldn't be as illuminated by the oncoming cars—if I was to be seen, I'd rather the police got a good look at my ass.

I'd walked about a mile or so before a small truck slowly passed me and came to a stop. I made a quick should-I-start-running appraisal of the situation. It wasn't the cops—unless they started using mini-trucks as squad cars. I kept my pace. The truck reversed. A window rolled down and a woman's voice catcalled me from the dark interior.

"Are you working, Baby? You're looking mighty fine."

I didn't acknowledge her. I kept walking.

"I'm talking to you, Sugar Stick. You looking for fun?"

I stopped and turned toward the truck. I'd had enough. Gracie stuck her head out the window.

"You want a ride?"

I was glad to see her, but a feeling of pride stood between us—I had made it this far.

"Nah, I'm cool. Thanks for stopping but…I like walking and…uh…"—*it was a long way back. I may be a prick, but I'm not stupid. I've got blisters on my feet—pride took a backseat to comfort*—"You know, I think I will take a ride. I'm fucking out here, huh?"

"Sweetie, there's nothing on this road but coyotes and prostitutes—you could have been bit by either one."

Gracie opened the door and slid over. I climbed in. Hank was at the wheel. The motel man grunted a curt "Hello."

"What the fuck are you guys doing out here?"

"We're coming from a meeting—a group of ex-drunks, you interested?"

"In being an ex-drunk? No. I'm doing okay."

"Is that what you think?" said Hank.

"Hey, fuck you, man"—I leaned over Gracie. She pushed me back.

"Come on, Hank, let it go."

The desk clerk had his eyes on the road—"I was just fucking around—having some fun."

"Well, some people shouldn't be fucked with."

Gracie squeezed my thigh—"He's just being Hank, and you"—she tossed my hair—"should be nicer to your saviors."

"Yeah, I guess you're right. Sorry, man, rough night."

"S'okay," Hank replied.

Gracie ran her middle finger across the back of my neck. "You still didn't tell me what you were doing out here."

"I was running."

"In that outfit?"

"It's all I had. I stopped about a mile ago and I was just walking back—no big deal."

Hank didn't let it go. "You're about five miles out, guy."

I bristled again and Gracie calmed me with a laugh.

"Anyway," she said, "I'm glad we saw you."

"Ask him, Gracie. You know he's done it."

"Done what?" I replied.

"Hank and I were just talking about getting so drunk that you forget where you parked the car, so you call the police and tell them it was stolen."

"Ha! I ride a bike, but yeah—I've lost it a few times. I try not to ride now—at least when I'm drinking."

"Oh," Gracie giggled, "so you're controlling and enjoying?"

"Yeah," said Hank, "well, I think she got fucked up and faked the whole thing. I once told my boss that my crazy ex tied me to the bed as I slept—he bought it."

"Maybe she's headed to rehab, and the whole thing was just a way to save face."

I was clueless—either that or I'm losing it— "What the fuck are you guys talking about?"

"Abigail Dupree—Hank and I think she concocted the whole thing."

"What thing?"

"Where have you been?" said Gracie. "She went missing a few days ago."

"I know she's missing—I'm not a fucking idiot."

"You didn't know they found her."

"You shit-talking me, Hank?"

"Easy, killer. She walked into a police station this

afternoon—it's in the late edition"—Gracie handed me the evening paper—'It's right there—front page, bottom right—heiress found."

"What the fuck?"

"I think she's full of shit," said Hank. "She probably went on a bender and lost her car—fuck. I've been fucked up for a week or two and had no idea where I was—shit, one time I hijacked a fucking bakery truck; I was rolling down the street throwing donuts at handicapped kids and getting all fucking loose…"

I drifted into thought as Hank rolled into a long drunkelogue.

When we pulled into the Sundowner parking lot, I could see Burroughs sitting in a chair by our door. He was smoking.

Gracie walked over and gave the old man a quick hug—"Look what we found"—she pulled at my arm—"he was hooking."

Burroughs laughed—"I sure hope not!"

"We caught him before he could get to it"—Hank wiggled his ass. Gracie pushed the desk man and sent a soft kick to his rear—"Why don't you get to work, Trixie."

Hank walked to the office. I hung back.

"All right, gentlemen," said Gracie, "I'm off to bed"—she touched my arm as she passed—"and why don't you stay within the perimeter. Good night."

Burroughs reached into his jacket pocket and pulled out another cigar—"Smoke with me?"

I felt like a little boy—embarrassed, standing before my grandmother, ashamed of my behavior, struggling to speak.

"I'm sorry."

"It's okay, Arthur, it's my fault. I shouldn't have slapped you"—the old man stood up and put his arms around me.

I returned the hug and let him hold me longer than was comfortable. Finally—like my sweet little Frank, I wriggled free.

"They found Abigail."

"I know, I was just reading about it"—Burroughs sat down

and tapped the newspaper on his knee—"I'm relieved, but…what does this mean for you and me?"

"You're sounding like me now, Mr. B. 'I know the world's coming to an end, but what about me?'"

I lit the cigar and took a hit—*The old man wasn't cheap when it came to tobacco—this smoke was no exception—a nice, imported stick*—"You know. I don't think I knew how much I really cared until I heard she was found—I didn't even know I was carrying it, but man—a load sure came off."

Burroughs looked over the parking lot. "Arthur, where's the van?"

"I traded it."

"It's in my name, you idiot. Where is it?"

"It's not gone for good—"

"—It shouldn't be gone at all!"

"Terry has it—he's cool."

"T. Terry—the drug dealer? Are you out of your mind?"

I told my interrogation story to Burroughs. He wasn't impressed when I flashed my cut hand.

"I saw the cuts earlier. I figured you'd been busy—but I had no idea you were horse-trading. We need to go pick that van up—and don't give me that crap about him being cool with the theft of his vehicle because you popped him in the face—or are you trying to add strong-arm robbery to your list of wants?"

"Jesus, man—it's your fault, I told you to get that fucking Maserati. If we get in a chase in that piece of shit van, we're done for—hey, how was Frank?"

"I didn't get there."

"Why not?"

"Because I was busy finding out where you came from. I did in one day what Social Services couldn't do in a year."

"You could've gone afterwards."

"Yeah, I could've, but I didn't. I think your Frank will be alright getting his dirty sock tomorrow."

"Frank...fuck"—*as I recalled my boy, I thought of my twin*—"that cocksucker is the same name as my little man, that's fucked up."

"That 'cocksucker' is your brother, and you probably named the cat subconsciously."

"Yeah, but I don't wanna think of him, when I think of him—you know what I mean?"

"And your mother probably called him Frank, so she wouldn't have to think of your father."

"Well let's all change our fucking names then. You can be...Vladimir, and I'll be Viktor—Viktor the Victorious!"

Burroughs laughed—"Arthur—or should I say, Count Viktor, you do make being a fugitive fun."

CHAPTER SEVENTEEN—GOING DOWN

A bottle broke on parking lot pavement. A door slammed. An engine choked into life.

I went to the window as a pair of taillights pulled out of the lot. I checked on Burroughs; the old man was still asleep. I dressed and stepped outside. I wasn't sure of the time, but it felt like an early morning or an extremely late night. I walked past the closed doors of empty motel rooms until I came to a pile of freshly broken glass.

"What a fucking waste"—I picked up a large shard of an alcohol sodden bottle and held it beneath my nose—*sloe gin. No wonder they dropped it*—I closed my eyes and inhaled—"I'd say, two teenagers drinking gin fizzies and giving each other herpes."

"More like a creepy old man—sipping it straight as he makes out with a blow-up doll."

I turned to see Gracie holding a dustpan and a broom. She was wearing a light powder-pink pajama set and a pair of men's beige work boots—"I saw him drop the bottle as he was putting her in the car."

I laughed and helped Gracie clean up the broken glass.

"You're up early."

"I guess the noise woke me"—I checked my imaginary watch—"what are we looking like?"

"It's looking like a little after 4am—I was about to do my morning meditation when I saw him leave—you always up this early?"

"Never, but then again, things are kinda on their heads right now"

"Do you wanna come in for a coffee or are you going back to bed?"

"Yeah, that sounds nice."

"What, bed or coffee—or both?"

"I'll take bed and coffee for $400 please."

"$400? You're taking that hooking thing seriously aren't you? I might be able to come up with a scone, but I'm short on hard cash."

"That's okay. I'll sell my ass for a pastry."

Gracie's place was nice. It was much larger than our number twelve. There was an alcove with an unmade queen bed and the kitchen was of decent size. Candles were lit and placed throughout. The air was infused with incense.

"I like that"—I waved my hand through the smoke—"it smells nice."

"It's Tibetan—I don't buy that crap off the street—it gives me a headache, and you don't know what's in it."

"Ah, so you disdain black market tranquility"—I checked out her room—"Is the gong legit?"

"It's a dark witch spirituality kit. I got it at Sears."

She filled up a kettle of water and placed it on the stove—"Do you like light roast or dark?"

"I like it dark—hot, bitter, and black."

"I'm not bitter, you prick"—she laughed as the burner came to life—"I blew out that back wall and added that room. It's a small space, but I don't need much—less things, less headache."

She took her boots off and placed them by the door. Her socks matched her pajamas.

"I like your boots."

"Yeah, they were the best part of an old boyfriend—I kicked him to the curb and kept the shoes."

She took out a French press and scooped in the coffee—the scent of freshly ground beans pleased me—"You getting fancy? I usually drink my coffee at the diner—nothing special. You know, I was gonna open a breakfast place."

"Really?"

"Yeah, just breakfast—a very limited menu—I had a name and everything."

"What were you going to call it?"

"Cop Breakfast."

"What does the C.O.P. stand for?"

"It stands for cop—as in cop, you know—the Big Blue Gang—the Corporation. I was gonna serve a jelly donut, a Marlboro red, and a cup of Folgers—that's their standard go-to. I even had a sign sketched out—three pigs without pants, wearing police jackets and hats, smoking and eating donuts."

"Was there going to be a kid's plate?"

"Nah"—I caught her jest—"adults only"—I sat on her bed— "Do you mind?"

"No, of course not."

"Yeah, maybe one day. I bet it'd go over really well around here."

"Were you an officer, Arthur?"

"Me? No. Well...one night I was, but that's not my thing— I like to see people pay for their crimes, but I'm not a fan of cages. I'm a private investigator."

She poured two cups and handed me one. "It's not Folgers— but it is hot and black."

She took off her pajama top and got in bed. Her chest was scarred and flat—she caught me checking her out.

"They asked me if I wanted reconstructive surgery, but fuck it, why should I? I know who I am, and it's not a set of tits."

I took a sip of coffee—it was just as I liked it.

"I've never been a tit man. I don't understand it—here little boy, come suckle mommy as you jerk off—kinda creepy, yeah?"

She laughed as she lifted a corner of the blanket—"You getting in?"

I kicked off my shoes and took off my shirt—"Pants too?"

"I'm not going to fuck you, if that's what you're thinking, but yeah—unless you have multiple black slacks in your suitcase; you've been wearing that pair for a few days—they're probably filthy."

I took off my pants.

"Nope, just as I thought—same little bikini too."

"I haven't had a chance to shop."

"At least you have nice legs."

I got in bed and she flipped the covers up.

"So, what kind of man are you?"

"What kind of man?"

"You said you weren't a tit man—"

"Oh, for me it's the eyes—I guess if I was to fall in love with someone, it'd be because of where they've been, not what they came in—although, I do like your vehicle."

"What'd they used to call it when a car was old and clean?"

"A cream puff."

"Yeah, a cream puff, I'm not."

I caressed her face—brushed back her hair.

"Have you known Tom long?" she said.

"Yeah, he was friends with my grandmother—I've known him for most of my life."

We sat quietly for a moment.

"This is nice, Gracie."

"Yeah"—she kissed me—"it is."

I pulled slightly away from her—"Do you wanna know what I'm doing here?"

"I figured if you wanted to tell me, you would, and if not, I wasn't going to ask."

"I'm working with Burroughs on a case."

"Well, that's better than what I thought."

"Yeah, what'd you think?"

"I thought you were a snitch."

"A snitch—what the fuck?"

"Yep, Hank said, 'mob stoolie'"—she smiled—"you do kind of look the part."

"Fuck Hank—and you found me being a snitch attractive?"

"Who said I found you attractive?"—she teased my leg with her foot—"And anyway, maybe I have a thing for rats."

"I'm not a rat—I'm being framed for a murder I didn't commit."

"Oh, a killer"—she exposed her neck and closed her eyes—"Hurt me, Arthur."

"Do you think that's funny?"

"No. I just don't think you're dangerous—at least, not to me"—she set her coffee on a small table by the bed, rolled toward me, and traced my stomach with her hand—"I do believe you're a killer though—you have it in your eyes, but I don't think you're evil—or should I say, wantonly murderous"—she let her hand drop to my crotch—"although…this does feel dangerous."

"I thought you weren't gonna fuck me."

She took the coffee cup out of my hand and set it on the table.

"I'm not. You're going to go down on me—I'm going to lay here and enjoy it."

She pulled her pajama bottoms off her hips, and I slid down between her legs. I pulled at her panties, but she refused their removal.

"No, lick me through the cotton. I don't know what you might be carrying. That mouth looks dirty."

She winked, pushed my head down, and then she leaned back into the pillows.

"You're a good boy, Arthur—make mommy cum."

I knocked on the door with my foot. Burroughs opened it— I handed the old man a coffee.

"Where were you?" he said.

"I was with Gracie—that bitch is crazy."

"Did you sleep with her—wait, I don't want to know."

I flopped down in the chair; my coffee splashed my pants— "I need a change of clothes."

"You need a bath—you smell like a Hindu whorehouse."

I smelled my shirt—*it wasn't that bad.*

"Arthur, get yourself cleaned up, and then we'll get our day together—you do know you're still in the shit."

I crept safari style towards the bathroom—"I'm deep in the dark bush, bwana. Ha!"

The water was hot, and as my body became accustomed to the heat, I made it hotter until my skin became red. I inhaled the steam and took deep cleansing breaths—*at home, I often stand in the shower until the water becomes cold.*

Burroughs pounded on the bathroom door—"Hey, can we get going here?"

I dried off and wrapped the towel around my waist. My underwear were beyond dirty—unbearable.

"Fuck, Tom; seriously, I need a change of clothes."

"Turn them inside out."

"Did you really just offer that as a solution? I hope to fuck you're not doing that"—I sniffed the air, and then tossed my used briefs into the small bathroom wastebasket—"I'm going without, but I need something today—you had a chance to change."

"I saw a Jumbo-Mart off the highway, we could go there."

"Does this look like Jumbo-Mart?" I ran my hands down my

tailored wool slacks—a coffee stain near the crotch—"I get these from Roscoe's on Broadway. I'm not wearing bargain rags."

"That's wonderful, Arthur, why don't we stop by there and tell Roscoe that you need a whole new wardrobe—maybe something from his killer-on-the-run collection—a nice wool gabardine."

"You don't gotta be a smartass. We could call ahead."

"Yes, please call ahead," Burroughs teased, "warn him that we're coming."

"I hear you. Look, when you go to Matsudo's for the key, just grab some of my clothes—no big deal."

"Do you wear condoms, Arthur?"

"What the fuck does that gotta do with this?"

"Do you?"

"No."

"That's what I thought. I'm the only safe one in this duo."

"Oh, don't tell me you're still fucking."

"What I'm telling you is; we're not going to Roscoe's, and I'm not walking out of your building with a suitcase or a bag stuffed full of your finery. If someone happens to be casing the joint, they'll know I'm in contact with you. So put your goddamn shoes on and let's go. I'm sure you can find something at Jumbo-Mart that'll work for you. Who knows, they might even have a picky-little-punk section."

The Jumbo-Mart was as I figured—it was where the bottom of the gene pool shopped. There were cast-off dirty diapers in the aisles and Battle Flag ice-coolers on end-cap displays. I stood distraught in the middle of the men's department.

"Seriously, Tom, feel this—it's like putting burlap on your balls. You want me to wear these?"

"Arthur, if you don't like it here, then go to the women's department and get your panties there"—he grabbed me by the arm and steered me toward two hideously dressed female mannequins—"It's taken you almost an hour to pick out two pairs of slacks, a couple shirts, and a cowboy hat—which, for the life of me, I have no idea what you need that for."

"It's for the Mustang"—I flipped the hat onto my head and struck a pose—"You know this is bad ass."

"Let's get you some silk panties, Hoss."

Another half hour passed before I was satisfied.

"These are going to feel nice on—here, check this"—I rubbed the panties on Burroughs cheek.

"Arthur, get your God damn—"

"Hold up, Mr. B."

"What's going on?"

"It's Paul—at the checkout"—I turned to a saleswoman at the layaway desk and spoke like a high school girl—"Could you please hold these for us? Daddy forgot his wallet—we'll be right back."

"Of course"—the woman smiled at Burroughs—"I'll put your name on them…"

"His name is Ricky."

"What are you doing—and what's this daddy business?"

"We're gonna tail that little fuck."

"Are you sure it's him? You do know there are many little people of color."

"That's him—the fucking midget with a ten-inch prick. What do you want me to do, yell, 'Hey, Paul?'"

"No, I just want you to be sure before we run off half-cocked."

"Fully—cocked—that little fucker is packing large."

We hung back until the little man had made his purchases, and we followed him outside. He was pushing a shopping cart of cleaning supplies. He stopped behind a gold Cadillac and popped open the trunk.

"I fucking told you—little people of color, my ass. The

world ain't full of midgets, my man. That's him—guaranteed. Let's get the fucking car."

We jumped into Burroughs' rental and drove to an open corner of the Jumbo-Mart lot. We watched Paul pull out, then we tucked ourselves neatly behind him.

"What the fuck is he doing out here?"

Burroughs remained cautious—"Why wouldn't he be here?"

"Because I know where they shoot—him and Heavy got a warehouse near Little Italy—the Dick Palace—fucking creeps, man—can you believe they actually call it that? 'Hey, Baby, why don't you come on over to the Dick Palace and have a cup of cocoa'—ugh! He's got no reason to be out here."

We followed the gold Cadillac until it came to rest in front of an old storefront. I put my seat all the way back. "Drive by— what's he parked behind?"

"A red Corvette."

"That's Dick Heavy's ride—those fuckers are like crabs—if you see one of 'em, you know there's another."

"What should we do?"

"We're gonna go back and get that fucking cowboy hat—I'll catch these pricks later."

I stood in front of the mirror in my new sheer panties.

"Well, how do they feel?" said Burroughs.

"They feel all right, but why is it that when you put on women's clothes, it seems like you're being naughty? I mean—it's not like the cut is that much different."

"Arthur, could you please get dressed now? Frankly, your impromptu fashion show is starting to get a little weird."

"Oh, look who's all 'hung-up'"—I put my new pants on and buttoned my Jumbo-Mart shirt—"Hey, do me a fucking favor—if I get pinched, please make sure I've got decent trousers—these are a fucking embarrassment."

"Sure"—Burroughs adjusted his collar—"'Your Honor?

Could you please hold the arraignment, I need to run over to Roscoe's and get my client a nice suit'—sweet Jesus, Arthur. Now look here—pay attention, I think you should check out Dick Heavy and Paul—keep the violence to a minimum, and I'll go pick up the locker key."

"And give Frank the sock?"

"Yes, of course. I'll give Frank the sock."

"Where is it?"

"It's in the glove box, God damn it. I'm not going to walk around with that dirty thing in my pants pocket."

"And what about Abigail?"

"I was going to stop by the hospital and feel her out."

"Can I go?"

"To the hospital? Of course not."

"I know I can't go in—I mean, can we go together? I don't wanna drive around alone. Let me go with you?"

"Are you serious?"

"Yeah—I don't wanna be alone—I'm feeling a bit sketchy. I promise I'll keep it low key."

"You're going to be doing a lot of waiting."

"It's okay. I need time to think"—I put on my cowboy hat and adjusted it in the mirror.

"What are you doing with that hat?"

"I'm driving. We're taking the Mustang."

CHAPTER EIGHTEEN—THIS AIN'T BULLIT

I lit up the big green Mustang and revved the engine—"Finally, a fucking action plan. Let's get it, Baby!"—I punched the gas and spun the tires—a quick Goodyear chirp on the pavement.

"Arthur!"—Burroughs latched on to the roof handle—"I think this is a bad idea."

"What the fuck? Are you kidding? We haven't even pulled out of the lot—I'll mellow out. I'm just fucking around."

"Just stop—please."

I put the Mustang in reverse and backed into a parking stall—"What's wrong?"

"I don't know. Maybe I'm just spooked"—Burroughs took off his seatbelt—"I'm not feeling right about this."

"Come on, man. You're not the superstitious type."

"You're right, I'm not. What I'm feeling is called a hunch—some of them good, and some bad, but let's take it as I first planned. You check out that storefront, and I'll go see Abigail and Matsudo."

"Seriously? You're gonna split on me?"

"Yes, and please, check it out easy—don't roll over there being all, 'Arthur.'"

"What the fuck does that mean?"

"It means that I don't want to come back to a bloody sink."

I turned off the engine, and Burroughs got out of the car. The old man, without looking back, climbed into his rental and drove off.

"Well, I'm glad he's satisfied."

I swung the rearview mirror in my direction and turned the radio on. I spun through the dial.

I never understood those cats that only liked one sound. Fuck, man, how boring is that? I like me some jazz in the late evening, some punk when I step out vicious, and when I'm in the bucket—feeling really down, a nice sugary pop tune to brighten up a dark day. I'm not monogamous when it comes to music—shit, I'm not monogamous at all, except for Frank, I'd never cheat on that little fucker—ha, that would be funny though; he comes in, and I'm lying in bed with a beautiful tabby—'I can't believe you, Arthur— you let her shit in my litter box, you bastard!'

I landed on a fun pop song. I cranked it up, and as I sang along, I checked my look in the mirror. It was good.

"I'm not talking about moving in, and I don't want to change your life..."

Gracie pounded on the driver's window. Unbowed, I turned toward her and finished the line.

"But there's a warm wind blowing, and the stars are out...and I'd really love to see you tonight."

I rolled the window down, but left the radio up.

"Hey, Tex. You wanna turn that shit down?"

"What's up?"—I slightly twisted the knob.

"Are you allowed to sit in the car when your parents aren't home?"

"Yes, I'm allowed."

"You're like a little boy out here. Where'd you get that hat?"

"Jumbo-Mart."

I hit the volume.

She reached in and turned it down.

With a loud exhale of air, I spun the knob hard to the right—the end chorus lit up the speakers and shook the windows.

She turned it down again—"Do it one more time and I'll bite your fucking hand off. What's the matter with you?"

"I feel lonely."

I told her that I was going to run errands with Burroughs, but that the old man thought better of it and told me to go alone.

"You probably blew his eardrums out. I'll go with you—if you want."

"You don't gotta work?"

"No. I've got a new girl on—it's never busy, but if she gets in trouble, she can wake Hank. Give me a second—do I need a gun?"

"What?"

"Don't you guys carry guns?"

"Some of us do, but not me—I usually carry a knife, but I lost mine."

"Damn, Arthur, I don't know why that turns me on—you carrying a knife, but my pussy's wet—ha! Give me a minute."

Gracie walked away as I rolled up the window, cranked up the radio, and rechecked my look in the mirror—*I was feeling better already.*

"Where are we going?" She put on her seatbelt and turned the radio down.

"I was thinking we could do some donuts in a parking lot, grab a bottle of sauce—oh, you don't drink, do you?"

"No, I don't—and neither do you, as long as you're behind that wheel. I thought you had business."

"I do. We're heading towards the airport—do you know that little strip there—I think it was called the Broker's Row?"

"Yeah, I used to pick-up down there."

"Huh?"

"Drugs, Arthur. Not a great memory."

"You still wanna go?"

"Well, you are cute, aren't you? I'm a big girl. My past doesn't scare me. Does yours?"

I thought of my father and the brother I was yet to know.

"It ain't good."

"No, I wouldn't think it was."

I took the Mustang through its paces and allowed Gracie control of the radio—"You don't get to switch the channel, but you can turn it up or down."

"That's fucking ridiculous. If I can't change the station, then I'm not in control."

"You control the volume—shit! Look out!"—I was forced to swerve—a beat up Towne Car was doing 25mph in the fast lane—"Fucking bitch, why are these people allowed on the road?"

Gracie cranked the volume to ten and buried me in sound. I turned it off.

"And that's what they call an operator override—when the controller is out of control."

"Your control, yes."

She put a foot up on the dash. Her long slender leg took my mind off the road. I stomped on the break—barely missing a concrete truck.

"Okay, legs down. We gotta focus here—"

"—You've got to focus."

"—This is serious shit"—I drove past the storefront; Paul's gold Cadillac was parked near the corner. There was no sign of Heavy's Corvette—"We're gonna swing around the back—we can't just park out front and saunter up to the door, as if we're pushing Bibles—this is the devil's business, young lady—besides, I'm not sure if they know this car."

"If who knows?"

"Paul and them—they might know Terry's car."

"Who, the fuck, is Terry? Is that your girlfriend?"

"He's a boy—I borrowed it yesterday. We need to be low-key."

"Yeah, and that cowboy hat and your heavy foot is getting it—maybe don't light it up around the corners—huh?"

"For your information, smart ass—look at this car—an asshole in a cowboy hat, driving like an idiot, fits it; if I was puttering around, it'd look suspicious."

"Oh my God. The fact that your logic seems sound, to me, is frightening."

We parked the car and walked down the main street. I held Gracie's hand—a couple of lovers window shopping—unassuming.

"Are we buying crack, Arthur—shopping for dope? I'm not sure if you looked around, but the Green, this place is not"—she lightly squeezed my hand—"Do we have a plan?"

"I prefer to work on instinct—let's just see what happens."

We were a few storefronts away when Paul and Jenny walked out of the shop. I pushed Gracie against the wall, turned my back toward the couple, and kissed her neck.

"Is this part of your instinct?" she said.

"That's my guy, Paul—and that's that bitch from the coffee shop—kiss me."

Gracie put her lips against mine and slightly opened her mouth—our tongues touched.

"Don't kiss me like that—Jesus. I'm not trying to roll up with a hard-on—fucking, Gracie. What are they doing?"

"It looks like they're getting in a cab—no, just the girl. The little dude grabbed her ass, and she hit his hand—that's it, she's leaving, he's heading back in."

I buried my face against Gracie's neck—let my hand slide up beneath her sweater. My eager fingers met the hard leather of a holster—"What the fuck? You're armed?"

"Yeah, I told you."

I stepped away and held open her sweater. She wore a form fitting shoulder holster properly concealed.

"Oh, that's fucking badass."

"Yeah, and sexy as fuck, too—a Walther P38."

"I want one."

"Really, I thought you were a knife slinger."

"Yeah, not your gun…the holster—I'd love to strap that on when I ride my bike—I mean, I'd get the gun to go with it, but I wouldn't conceal it"—I pretended to ride as I drew an invisible firearm from beneath my shoulder—"Where's your blinker, motherfucker—bam, bam, bam!"

"Yeah, that's just what you need. I think you better stick to a knife—So, what are we doing?"

"Burroughs said to check it out, and we did, but that's not good enough. I already knew he was over here. I need information."

"Shouldn't we do what Burroughs says?"

"No, I gotta hunch—some hunches can be good and…"—*I forgot the old man's line*—"Fuck it. You're gonna knock on the door, and when he opens it, I'll force my way in behind you."

"How many people are in there?"

"I got no idea—how many rounds does that piece hold?"

"Eight, but I'm not going to go in there blasting."

"I didn't say you had to, but I doubt there's more than seven people in there, so fuck it—if it goes bad, we're cool—pop, pop, pop. Don't trip. Come on"—I pushed Gracie toward the door.

"What if he doesn't answer?"

"Believe me, that little fucker is a real creep—some piece of black candy goes knocking on his door, and he'll run out of there with his dick in his hand. Go."

I stood out of view as Gracie knocked. No one answered. She knocked again—louder this time, but still no reply.

"Keep fucking knocking—he's in there—oh, fuck no!"

Three doors down, the dwarf exited a shop and cartoon hustled to his car. He entered the passenger door and ass hopped across the seat. I was quick after him, but as I reached the Cadillac, the little man pulled away from the curb. I punched the window glass as I called to Gracie.

"Shoot the motherfucker! Shoot him!"

He accelerated into traffic as I ran back to the Mustang—Gracie hot on my heels. We jumped into the car and immediately spun hard and took after him.

"Why didn't you shoot that prick?"

"Are you out of your fucking mind?"

"You could've done the window at least—fuck that fucking glass, man—how thick is that shit? Keep an eye out"—there was morning traffic—not too much, but the dwarf wasn't yet visible—"there...no...there—there he is."

His Cadillac was trapped behind two trucks at a red light. In a moment of panic, the little man drove over the curb and took to the sidewalk—knocking over a newspaper stand in the process.

"Arthur, stop! Stop!"

"We got him, fuck that!"

"The cops are on him!"

As Gracie spoke, I saw the black and white light him up. I pulled the Mustang to the side of the road and parked out of casual view.

"Are you fucking kidding me? This is bullshit! What's with the fucking cops in this town? Are they just waiting for shit to do? Did you ever see Bullitt?"

"The movie?"

"Yeah, the fucking movie—motherfuckers flying all over town—four-wheel-liftoffs in that fucking—this car, a car just like this, and there isn't a fucking cop in sight. But not in real life—in real life you got a fucking midget, jumping the motherfucking curb, and in a second, it's 5-0 all over his fucking ass. I swear to fuck, if they take that little fucker in, I'm gonna raise hell. I'll lodge a formal complaint."

Gracie put her back to the door, and in silent disbelief, listened as I rambled on about the injustices of street life.

"What are they doing now?" I said. "Can you see 'em?"

"Yeah, I can."

"Are they arresting him?"

"No. It doesn't look like it."

"Why not?"

"How the fuck do I know?"

"You said you could see 'em."

"I can't hear what they're saying—calm down, you fucking psycho."

"That's not nice, Gracie."

She squeezed my thigh—"He's talking to 'em. It doesn't look like they're arresting him."

"Oh, that's right—fucking midget goes on the sidewalk, knocking over shit all over the place, and it's 'okay,' but you can bet—if it was me, a semi-straight, white man in America, I'd be getting cuffed up and beaten with a fucking nightstick."

"I'm gonna beat you with a fucking nightstick if you don't shut the fuck up."

"Okay—I'm shut, just keep watching."

"They shook his hand—they're letting him go."

"—A fucking travesty of justice."

"Make up your fucking mind, Arthur. One minute you want him free, the next—hang on, they're heading back to their car."

I tapped on the steering wheel, turned the radio on, turned it off, and tapped on the wheel again.

"Okay, he's back in the Caddy—pulling out—go easy."

I merged into traffic and resumed my slow chase. There was a bakery truck between us and I was able to use it for cover. We drove through the business section and toward the train yards. The road ahead was less traveled—a short tunnel under an overpass. Hopefully he'd turn onto the interstate before we hit that stretch. The bakery truck flashed its right blinker.

"If your little friend stays straight, our cover is gone"

I didn't reply.

"Hey, did you hear me? What are you going to do?"

The truck turned off; the Cadillac continued on; we were immediately spotted. The little man jumped on the gas. I followed suit. I stayed intent on the road—there was a slight bend ahead.

"Arthur?"

"I'm gonna ram that little fucker. Hang on!"

I punched it, downshifted, and as we picked up speed, I slammed into the right rear panel of the Cadillac. The big gold land-yacht spun into the overpass wall and came to a hard stop in the tunnel. I blocked his exit.

"Got him!"—I jumped out of the car—"Get behind the wheel."

Gracie crawled over the stick shift and into the driver's seat. I ran to the Cadillac, pulled open the driver's door, and kicked the stunned little man in the face. I repeatedly punched the dwarf—knocking him out as I worked my way into the car.

With Paul's body now slumped against the passenger door, I tried to get comfortable behind the wheel. The little man had installed extension blocks on both the brake and the gas pedals, so I was forced to drive with my knees to my chest. I backed the Cadillac off the wall, and we limped down the street.

There was a storage yard on my right—it looked unattended. I pulled in and parked behind a makeshift wall of empty freight containers. I exited the vehicle and dragged the dwarf into a large open metal box—its current occupant, an unpleasant transient, was less than pleased.

"Hey—what the fuck, guy? I'm in here!"

"Here's what the fuck"—I tossed Paul into a corner. His lolling head banged against the wall—"you're evicted, scumbag. Get the fuck out."

Gracie peeked into the container as the hobo gathered his things. I escorted him past her—ignoring his protests.

"Watch this fucker—I don't want him setting up shop in the Mustang."

As Gracie followed the transient to the street, I pinned the dwarf against the corner in a seated position. He was bleeding from his nose and mouth—his left eye was swollen shut. He was conscious, but not all there. Gracie returned as I was urinating on the little man.

Fuck, what do want out of me—he ran, and I caught him. So, what, I bit—it's not my fault—it's fucking nature, man. Even a poodle—a sweater wearing rhinestone'd faggot of a dog will nip you if you run from it—don't be so fucking judgmental—everyone knows, if you run, you get a beating. He shouldn't have ran.

"We're gonna have to wait a minute, I might'a gone a little hard on him."

"Is he alive?"

"Yeah, fuck—he's bleeding. I think it stops when they die, unless it just leaks out"—I put my hand over Paul's nose and mouth. I held it tight. The dwarf shook his head—"Yep—still alive. Where'd you park?"

"On the turn out."

"Were you careful of glass and nails?"

"Arthur, you fucked that car up."

"Well, we don't need a flat too, do we?"

Gracie poked Paul's crotch with her boot—"What'd he do to you?"

"He, uh…well…I'm not exactly sure. That's why we're here—to find out what he knows—interrogate him."

Paul was coming around.

"Arthur, you can't do this to people. He could be innocent."

The dwarf stared at Gracie as she spoke—his eyes widening to her compassion.

"He's not innocent. He drugged and raped Abigail Dupree, and then he and his fucked-up co-star, tried to extort her."

"Oh."

"Yeah, oh. Do you honestly think that I'm just randomly beating on dwarves? That's it, 'Hey, Gracie, would you like to go on a dwarf beating date, I got an itch?'"—I grabbed Paul by the hair—"This motherfucker is one hundred percent in on something and I'm gonna find out what it is—I already know what he did to Abi and that's more than enough for what he's getting. If you don't feel like watching, you can wait in the car because I am gonna hurt this little fucker—I'm going to hurt him real bad."

Paul mumbled through bleeding lips, "Don't leave me with him."

I licked my knuckles—"You'd better shut the fuck up, Paul."

"Please Ma'am, he'll kill me."

I kicked him in the stomach. The dwarf threw up on his chest—"Ugh, what'd you eat? Is that a cannoli?"—I took off my shirt and began to remove my pants.

"Arthur, what are you doing?"

"I don't want blood and cannoli all over my new clothes"— I handed my shirt and slacks to Gracie and then I loomed over the dwarf in my new women's panties.

"Are you going to kill him?"

"Let's just say, I'm not gonna be too broken up about it if he dies. Okay, Paul. How do you want it—easy or hard?"

"I don't want it."

"Yeah, well, you're gonna get it. This is what happens to creepy little dwarves that run around like big boys."

I put my foot on Paul's ample crotch and mimed a cigarette grind with my heel. The dwarf groaned and clutched at my leg.

"Hey, Gracie, you wanna see a ten-inch cock?"

"Maybe later, Arthur."

"Easy or hard, Paul—that is not a rhetorical question. I'm giving you an option."

"Easy! Fuck, Arthur, come on."

"Easy is not how I like it, but we'll see how it goes."

I grabbed the little man by his ears, and I lifted until his neck was stretched—"Why were you running?"

"Terry told Heavy what you did to him. He said you were coming for me."

"That piece of shit—I told him not to tell anyone."

"Heavy said you stole T's car—when I saw you through the window, I ran."

"Hmmm—and why would I be after you?"

"Cause you're a fucking maniac, man. How the fuck do I know why?"

"That's a real shitty answer, Paul—Gracie, will you get me that piece of pipe over there?"

The dwarves eyes widened—"Arthur, please—I'd tell you if I knew. I don't"—he began to choke.

"Do you need to spit?"—I released my grip on his hair. The dwarf slumped over and spit out a mouthful of blood. Gracie handed me the pipe.

"Thanks, Baby"—*she was sweet*—"you know, you make me wanna be a better man. Ha!"—I held the length of pipe like a golf club and I faced Paul—"So, before I tee-off on your head, I'd like you to talk to me about John Hawthorne and those terrible photos—and frankly, Paul, this container smells like essence of hobo and it's making me feel a bit ill, so I'd like to vacate this box as soon as we can."

"We shot the Dupree stuff, yeah, and I'm sorry, man, it was for the money. Hawthorne offered us a nice chunk of cash to fuck her and roll, and we did it. I thought the girl was down at first—freaked me the fuck out, man—being who she is and everything. She's standing there and then a second later she's on her knees swallowing my cock. I was a load into her before I realized that she might be out of it. It was wild, man—she isn't right, or Hawthorne wasn't lying about that blue sauce. I don't know. She seemed drugged—had that far-away look in her eyes, but then I heard her talking straight to him as if she was clean, and then she's back to riding my tool like a fucking porn star. It reminded me of high school—little girls acting all drunk so they had an excuse for being sluts."

"Hold up. I'm not interested in your Wizard of Oz high school confidential—was she drugged or not?"

"I don't know. Hawthorne was talking big about this new thing—like he was going to take over the fucking pussy trade with it—maybe she was on it—maybe she wasn't—who knows?"

"There are plenty of girls that don't need to be drugged to play. Why would he need that?"

"Yeah, that's what Dick said too, but Hawthorne had some fantasy of fucking society girls—turning 'em out. He said there was big money in it, and he had the means and the Hypno to make it happen—he's a fucking tool."

"The Hypno?"

"The drug, man. That's what he was calling it."

"But you didn't see Abigail take it?"

"No—if she was on something, she did it before they arrived."

"Alright—and now...me, how the fuck am I in this?"

Paul turned to Gracie—"Please don't let him hurt me."

"Why would I hurt you? Are you not playing nice?"

"Because I don't know. I got no fucking idea why you're here—if you were seeing the girl—I didn't know that."

"Were you seeing her, Arthur?" said Gracie.

"No—of course not"—I put the pipe end against Paul's chest—"You shouldn't be starting rumors, Paul"—I pushed down. The dwarf screamed.

"Are you kidding me, Arthur? You dragged me into this because you're fucking some socialite?"

"Whoa, you wanted to come, and no; I'm not fucking her"— I glared at Paul—"Do you see what you started?"

"I didn't—fuck, man, I didn't know—I'm not saying you

were."

"See"—I smiled at Gracie—"he doesn't know what he's talking about"—I poked Paul with the pipe—"Now what about those shots of Nikki?"

"What shots?"

I stepped on the dwarf's leg and pushed towards the ground—"The shots of Nikki, the blonde, you little fucker—the ones of me doing her."

"No, man, if you were there, you'd know—"

"Arthur?"

"Gracie, stay out of it. This is where shit gets a little tricky, and I'll explain later"—I turned to Paul—"You guys didn't shoot Nikki?"

"No, no, man. Dick and I weren't there. Hawthorne asked us to set him up; he said he had someone big coming, and that we weren't ready for it. He paid us good money; we set up the lights and everything; we did it all, and then we split. When we came back...it uh..."

"—It what?" I cranked down on his leg...hard.

"It was a fucking mess, man—blood everywhere."

"What do you mean?"

"I mean it looked like somebody fucking died—it was a bloody fucking mess."

"And you didn't see anyone?"

"They were gone, dude—Dick fucking freaked."

"And when I get ahold of Heavy, is he gonna tell me the same tale—a bloody mess?"

I stepped back and spoke to Gracie, "Wait until you see this fucker—they should call these guys the Oreo dick twins—they got two feet of cock between 'em"—I turned back to the dwarf—"Where's Heavy, Paul?"

"You ain't gonna find him. He split town—got spooked—didn't wanna get caught up in a fucking snuff beef."

"A snuff beef?"

"Yeah—fuck, Arthur, you know us; we do porn, man; we don't fucking kill people."

"Why didn't you leave town?"

"I got a crippled wife, dude. I can't afford to split." The little man spit out another mouthful of blood.

"Is she full size, your wife? Ha, I'd fucking love to see that—a little ladder getting him all up on that pussy—hey, Gracie, can you hand me that rag?"

She picked up a dirty towel from the floor. I tossed it to Paul—"Here, wipe your face."

The dwarf smelled the towel and dropped it without wiping.

"What about Jenny—that little coffee bitch, how the fuck is she in this?"

"Dick found her, man—we shot her—made a tight little film. She's a nasty little bitch. Dick was doing her, but then, when Hawthorne came around, she moved up. Dick was all bent out of shape."

"What was she doing at your place?"

"Dropping off cash—Dick told Hawthorne that he had to sweeten it up—too much heat for too little money."

"And you got the dough?"

The dwarf reached into his pocket and handed me a wad of hundreds.

"Arthur, give the money back—you can't rob him."

"I'm not"—I split the cash evenly and handed a piece to Paul—"That's for your car and this stack is for Terry. Now, before we wrap this up, we've got two more little things to handle, the first; where can I find Hawthorne?"

"I don't know, man—it's not like we were hanging at his pad—maybe Jenny. She might know."

"Okay, I'll take that, and second; what am I going to do with your body?"

"Arthur!"

Gracie stepped between the dwarf and me—"What the fuck?"

"I can't let him go—Terry told me he wasn't gonna tell anyone, and look what he did—shit, he's my friend. What do you think this little fucker is gonna do?"

"Nothing, man! Fuck, Arthur, I swear. I'm not Terry. I won't say nothing to no one."

"What about Dick? You're not gonna tell him?"

"No, fuck Dick, man. I'm not saying nothing. I promise."

"Gracie? Do you believe him?"

She stood silent for a moment, and then she moved closer to Paul—"Give me your wallet."

"Are *you* gonna rob him? What the fuck? That's fucking cold."

Paul fished the blood-streaked wallet from his pants.

Gracie pulled out his license—"Is this current?"

"Yeah, still on Lime St. You can check it out."

"And your wife, she's there too?"

"Yes."

"All right then,"—she tucked his license in her pocket—"let him go."

"Are you sure?"

"Arthur, I think this little man is smart enough to know when he's catching a break—aren't you, Baby?"

"Yes. I promise."

I dropped the pipe on the ground—"See how sweet she is? Come on, Gracie. It looks like we're going for coffee. I sure hope you like burnt roast."

CHAPTER NINETEEN—CROSSTOWN CHATTER

"What the fuck is that noise?"

"Did you look at the car when you got in? You crushed the fender."

I pulled to the side of the road and surveyed the damage. The crushed fender was brushing against the wheel. I put my foot on the tire and yanked at the metal. It cleared, but barely.

"I think I've got it. The tire was rubbing against it."

"And it's all fixed now, right?"

"Of course not, but it'll get us to Terry's so we can get the van."

"I'm sure he'll be thrilled at your restoration efforts"—she turned the rearview mirror in her direction and checked her hair—being satisfied, she turned to me—"I wanna talk to you about what happened."

"When?"

"Just now."

"The wheel?"

"Don't play stupid—you know what I'm talking about. I've seen you pull it together when you want something. This I-don't-know-what's-going-on shit isn't gonna fly."

"I gotta mental condition."

"How long have you been using that—playing stupid, incompetent, so you can get over on people? I'll admit your lost little boy routine is strangely attractive, but I need to know where you're at."

"And I need to not get therapy when I'm taking care of business."

"All right, consider it tabled, but we've got a talk coming."

"And what about you? You sure handled that quite well."

"The wheel?"

"No, not the fucking wheel. You know what I'm talking about!"

"Oh, so you can focus."

"Fuck you, Gracie. Short of stopping me from killing him, I didn't hear you screaming in horror."

"And I didn't hear you caring enough about me to ask where I come from—or is it all about you, Arthur?"

"Well, one of us *is* wanted for murder, and the other one is…"

"A murderer."

"Huh?"

"Yeah, Arthur, straight up. I'm sure you've heard of the Night Hounds."

She was talking about the bane of underworld gangsters—a ruthless band of contract killers—sort of a modern-day Murder Inc. I'd never heard of a woman in their ranks, but, then again, thank God, I never had to deal with 'em. I preferred to keep 'em as ghosts in the darkness, not as impromptu therapists sharing a hot cup of the bitter black as we lounge in early morning nightwear.

"Yeah, I've heard of 'em. What about it, are you saying…"

"—I'm saying that busting heads, blowing out knees, and separating fools from their mortal coils isn't foreign to me. I just didn't think I'd be back at it."

"Well, you did just kind of watch—It's not like you laid into him."

"You're right, but I wanted to, and that's something I need to get my head around. Just don't take me for some bitch you picked up on the highway. I like you—maybe too much, too soon, but I'm willing to see where this goes. I'm thinking your adventure might be a means of atonement for me—although, I'm not sure if there's any difference in killing fools because they're evil or killing fools because they're standing in the way of evil, but I'm interested."

"Fuck—can't you just go back to the smiling, shit talking Gracie busting my balls?"

"Yeah, I can go back, but hopefully not too far. We'll see."

She turned up the radio, closed her eyes, and sang along with an old pop tune—"I love this—one of my favorites."

"I'd never scheme or lie, Bill, there's been no foolin'"

I slid closer to the door—placed her in my peripherals, but I couldn't help but joining in on the chorus.

"But kisses and love won't carry me, 'til you marry me, Bill."

"You're gonna have to knock."

"Why?"

"Because he probably won't answer if he knows it's me."

"Christ, Arthur, is anyone happy to see you?"

"Oh, as if people were always happy to see you—'Hello, who is it?' 'It's me, Gracie, I've come to kill you.'"

"Drop it, asshole."

"You drop it, and don't be mean. Wait until you meet my Frank. He's always happy to see me"—*I recalled the last time I was away from my boy; the grey was more interested in a dead rat than me*—"well, most times. He can be a bit finicky."

Gracie knocked on the door. A man's voice called from inside.

"Who is it?"

Gracie looked to me and shrugged her shoulders.

"It's Gracie?"

"We're not open."

"Say you're dropping off a car for me."

"I'm here to drop off a car—Arthur sent me."

From inside, a push-bar clicked and the metal door opened. T. Terry stood in the entranceway—both of his eyes were black—a bandage crossed the bridge of his nose.

"Fuck, this is a shock." He held out his hand for the keys.

I stepped into the doorway—"A shock that I brought it back, come on, man, that's not cool."

Terry recoiled and backed into the club. I pushed my way through the door. Gracie followed.

"I've got a gun, Arthur. You better stay back."

"What are you doing? I'm bringing you your car—don't be a dick."

Terry's eyes flashed wildly around the room—searching.

Gracie picked up a small pistol off the counter. She smiled at Terry—"Here it is"—she hefted the piece as if checking its worth, emptied the rounds, and handed me the unloaded gun.

"What the fuck, Terry?"—I passed him the empty pistol— "And seriously, you need to hold the gun in your hand when you answer the door. If someone was coming to kill you, you gotta be ready—isn't that right Gracie?"—I smiled at the terrified club owner—"Anyway, I'm sorry about the other day—I brought your car back; I need the van. I didn't put gas in the Mustang, but I didn't go too far, so I think you're cool."

I tossed Terry the keys, and then I held out my hand. He checked his pockets.

"I think I left the keys in it."

"They're in it? Fuck, Terry. That's not my van"—I walked

out to the vehicles; Terry and Gracie were close behind. I opened the van door and peeped the ignition—"They're here—fuck, someone could've taken it."

"I was just out for a second, I— oh, what the fuck, man? What did you do to my fucking car? Look at her!"

"It's not that bad. You're being a bit dramatic."

"Shit—shit—shit." Terry surveyed the Mustang as he shot dirty, disgusted glances my way.

"Come on, dude, it's just the front, and in all reality, it is your fault—if you hadn't called Heavy, Paul wouldn't'a run; so...I think there's a lesson in that."

"You fucked me, man."

"I did not. I brought money." I handed Terry the wad of hundreds. He quick counted the bills.

"Fuck, that's not gonna cut it."

"Use your insurance, brother; the bills are just a little—I'm sorry sweetener. I hope we can put all this aside and move on. I'm looking forward to another night at your place"—I nodded toward Gracie—"I think she'd really enjoy it."

Gracie got in the van.

"And, hey, check out that cowboy hat—I left it on the seat. It fits the car, man—you'll look like a real bad-ass."

There was a parking lot across the street from the coffee shop. It gave us a good view of the entrance.

"So, I take it you want me to go in?"

"Yeah, but I'm buying"—I fished a bloody hundred out of my pocket.

"Seriously?"

"I didn't steal it. I guess with the blood on it, it got stuck in there—finders' keepers, yeah."

"What do you want?"

"A coffee—black."

"Americano?"

"Black and bitter—keep that little bitch's lips off the rim."

Gracie shook her head as she exited the van.

I love the way she moves—fluid, sexy, and now that I know more about her—dangerous.

I climbed into the back seat and unbuttoned my pants. It took me a few moments to get comfortable, and then I got to it. Gracie returned too soon. She stuck her head through the window.

"What the fuck are you doing?"

I pulled my shirt down over my erection.

"I was tired."

"Tired of jerking off."

She set one of the coffees on the roof as she opened the door.

"Here"—she offered me the cup, but then she paused—"are your hands clean?"

"Just give me the fucking coffee. Was she in there?"

Gracie slid behind the wheel—"Please tell me you weren't fucking that."

"I wasn't—are you kidding me? What do you take me for, some fucking creep?"

She looked at my unbuttoned pants and the rise in my slacks—"Oh no, everybody jerks off in daylight parking lots. I was just about to tickle my button."

"Was she in there?"

"Yes. She was in there, and she's a fucking little brat. I don't know if she was talking to the manager, or whoever that was, but your little friend was bitching at some poor woman about the money she owed her."

"Was she working?"

"Not that I could tell."

I took a sip of coffee—"This is nice."

A cab pulled in front of the coffee shop. Jenny backed out of the business as she ran her mouth to whomever was inside.

"Here we go! You're driving."

Gracie pulled out after the cab.

"You know it's pretty roomy back here."

"Why don't you just keep your dick in your pants?"

The cab drove through the arts district and entered the waterfront loop. Gracie was steady and confidant behind the wheel. She remained adequately spaced and nondescript.

I liked my view from the back—"This bitch has no right coming into the harbor."

The cab turned onto Central. Gracie hung back and then made the turn.

"Fuck, we're going right by my place. I'll show you where I live—I wish we could stop in and see Frank."

The cab turned onto Broadway.

"Look to the right, as we go by—I live right there."

"Arthur, they're stopping."

"Shit, there's Burroughs' rental. Pull up behind 'em."

"No. Get your head down"—Gracie passed the office—"we have to be cool here."

"Oh, fuck that, we gotta back him up, warn him, or…"

"Exactly—we don't know what the fuck we need to do—trust me, Baby, just hang tight."

We pulled to the side of the road and looked out the back window of the van. Jenny exited the cab and went inside.

"Does Burroughs know this girl?"

"No…I mean, I don't think so."

"And he didn't expect you here?"

"No."

"Do you know what he's doing here?"

"Yeah, he's picking up a key and giving Frank a sock. Where are you going with this?"

"I'm going anywhere it could go. We've got to stay cool—he might know her; he might've planned this…"

"And he might be in trouble."

"Yeah, he might be, but we don't know, so—"

Jenny walked out of the building and hopped into

Burroughs' car. She did a U-turn and parked in front of the building.

"Come on! We've gotta go!"

"No! Wait."

As Gracie said wait, Burroughs walked out of the apartment closely followed by a dark-haired man.

"That's fucking Hawthorne!" I attempted to leave the van. Gracie grabbed my arm—"Sit the fuck down!"

Jenny reached over and opened the passenger door. The old man slowly climbed into the car. A gun became visible in Hawthorne's hand. He climbed in after Burroughs.

CHAPTER TWENTY—SURPRISE

"Fuck! I fucking told you"—I buttoned my pants and grabbed the door handle—fumbling to open it. Gracie grabbed my arm and blocked my exit.

"Arthur, who's in the house?"

"We've gotta go, man—"

She transferred her grip to the collar of my shirt holding me back—*a rabid beast on a leash struggling to run.*

"Arthur, focus! Listen to me—who's in the house?"

I hung on the edge of madness—"Frank and Matsudo."

She was cool—reining me in—"Are they important to you?"

The rental car pulled away from the curb.

"Yes, they're—fuck, come on, Gracie. They're leaving!"

She held my head in her hands, not letting me look towards the car—eyes locked on mine. She was stronger than I assumed.

"Okay, Arthur, you've got it—follow them, but don't engage unless absolutely necessary. I'll sort this out"—she jumped from the van—"Listen to me—is there a number you can reach me at?"

My heart and eyes were now locked in violent pursuit. She slapped me—hard—"Focus!"

I recoiled in anger, but didn't raise a hand to her—"Yes, I'll call Matsudo's. He's on the bottom floor."

She allowed me to pull away—"Don't panic, Baby—stay cool"—Gracie jogged toward the building as I went after Burroughs.

I wanted to force their car off the road—exact my vengeance, but against all instinct, Gracie's words and her sobering slap held me true. I felt a quick moment of gratitude for Burroughs' choice of low-key vehicle, as I often came into view, but then the thought of the old man suffering at their hands, turned my gratitude into a patient rage.

They led me through the garment district, and then we stopped in front of a warehouse in Chinatown. I watched as Jenny left the car. She lifted a roll-up, corrugated steel door, and then she got back inside the rental and drove in. The door closed behind them. I parked the van and walked toward the building.

I was conscious of my self—knowing that, if I was seen, my presence might put the old man in greater danger. I stood on the stoop of a shuttered dim sum bakery and caught my breath. There was a payphone on the corner—I knew Matsudo's number by heart, but I didn't feel that the time to report or check on Frank was now.

A light came on in a window above the warehouse—the second floor—accessible from the fire escape on the side of the building.

I realized, as I stood on that corner, that I had a lot to learn about self-control—I was hyperventilating—slow, Arthur, slow.

The girl came to the window; she looked down on the street. I leaned against the wall and cast my gaze to the ground.

To casual notice, I was a street creature with no intent or purpose. I felt bare without my knife, but a good animal can always find a handy tool.

A cab pulled up to the building and idled as it waited. After a few moments, a door next to the roll-up opened; Hawthorne and the girl walked out and approached the cab. He passionately kissed her—ran his hand over her ass, and then opened the door for her. It was a tender parting, and their casual display of affection sickened me.

Oh, so they like to play it cool, eh? Sweet kisses as my friend waits as a captive inside. I like cool too…well, cold really—nothing goes down easier than emotionless retribution—The cab drove off and Hawthorne returned inside—*I felt myself disconnect.*

I walked across the street and entered the small easement on the side of the building. I looked neither right nor left. I accessed the property as if I owned the place, and then I climbed up the fire escape to the second-floor window. My view of the room was limited—the window dirty, cracked and taped, but I could see Hawthorne and faintly hear his voice.

"What the fuck was I supposed to do," he said, "ask him politely for the key and the locker number?"

A voice answered—"You were supposed to do what I fucking told you—get the key, do everyone in the house, and get the fuck out."

"I did what I could. The fucking landlord was barricaded in his apartment—I kicked the hell out of the door, but no use; I had to do the phone lines, so he couldn't call out."

"Then you should have pressed Burroughs, got the info, and torched the place. You make me wonder why I keep you around; if it wasn't for your father, you'd be gone—do you understand?"

"Yes."

"Do you understand?"

"Yeah, Frank, I understand."

At the mention of Frank, I was down for attack, but I needed more.

"And there's something else I've been meaning to mention—you going into the porn business, Johnny?"

"Huh?"

"You know what the fuck I'm talking about; Abigail said you were drugging those rich cunts."

"Abigail is a fucking liar; she's full of shit."

"She knew enough to bail on you—thought your incompetence would bring her down. And now she's laying up in that hospital hotel waiting to see if you self-destruct."

"I'm doing the best I can, Frank—yeah, I got a little off base—chasing side money—we all do sometimes, but I'm on it."

"You're on it? Where's my brother?"

"Hey, the old man knows—he'll spill it."

"Hang on a minute—I'm taking this call."

When the voice disappeared, I realized that the conversation was on speaker mode—my brother was remote. Hawthorne walked across the room and through an open door.

Frank's voice returned. "You need to rap this shit up. Get what you can from Burroughs, find out where Arthur is, and then leave the old man's body on the warehouse floor. My people will be there in an hour."

Hawthorne ran back into the room.

"Do you hear me? Hello?"

"Yes, I heard you; I'm here. Burroughs is coming around; Jenny popped him pretty hard, I…"

"—Jenny? Who the fuck is Jenny?"

"She's uh…"

"Listen to me, you incompetent piece of shit—is she still there?"

"No, but she'll be right back."

"Good, because I want two bodies; hers and the old man's, or his body and yours—take your pick. You've got an hour."

Hawthorne slammed the phone down and walked back into the adjoining room. I removed the window screen and climbed inside. The living room was sparsely furnished, cheap—not tidy.

I expected that of him—pretty on the outside and trash beneath—thankfully, I'm pretty through and through.

There was a small kitchen to my right. It was also filthy.

A sharp knife could make things...easier. I'm sure they've got a cutlery drawer 'round here.

There was a half-spent bottle of booze on the counter—Cutty Sark and a couple cans of warm cola.

I guess you don't realize how parched you are until you stand before a fountain and crave a drink—fuck, maybe a quick hit...a little something to wet the whistler.

I returned to the moment and pulled open a kitchen drawer.

Alright, here we go, not my weapon of choice, but it has been proven to be reliable.

I took a quick hit off the Cutty and crept back into the living room with a claw hammer in my hand. I approached the door and looked into the other room. Hawthorne had his back turned. Burroughs was tied to a chair—his head slumped down upon his chest.

"Fuckin-a," said Hawthorne, "she really popped you, huh; that little girl has a powerful swing, eh, old man?"

I edged toward the pair—breathless, soundless.

Hawthorne grabbed Burroughs' shirt and pushed him back—his head lolled to the side—"You still with us, fucker?"

I was close enough to smell his sweat—"Yes, I am."

Hawthorne turned to the sound of my voice.

"Frank, I uh"—as he saw the hammer clenched in my hand, he realized that he'd made a grave identity mistake—"Arthur."

"Yeah, you got it, Baby. Arthur—that's me."

Hawthorne held up his hands—arrest style.

"Hit the floor, asshole—NOW." *I raised my voice, but inside, I was calm as a midsummer day.* He dropped to the ground.

"Now place your hands on top of your head."

Hawthorne, with almost robotic precision, followed my commands.

"I didn't mean anything—I can get you money, big money."

I put my hand over his mouth—"Shut up"—I turned to check on Burroughs. His breathing was ragged, but steady. It looked as if they'd broken his nose. I momentarily turned back to Hawthorne and displayed a crooked evil smile.

"Tom"—I touched Burroughs' hand—"can you hear me?"

The old man opened his eyes, recognized me, and then closed them again. Tears trailed unabashed down his cheeks. I untied the old man's bonds and helped him to a small bed that was in the corner of the room. I then returned to Hawthorne, grabbed his shirt, and pulled him to his feet.

"I did what I was told," Hawthorne pleaded, "your brother…"

"Put your hands behind your fucking back"—I secured his wrists using the ties they had on Burroughs. "If you speak again, I'll kill you." I touched Burroughs shoulder—"Tom, I'll be right back—hang tight. It's gonna be okay."

Hawthorne I grabbed by the back of his neck and walked him from the room—"I'm sure you realize that this isn't gonna go well for you."

He opened his mouth to speak—

"—No, no—remember what I told you—you utter one word—one weak, little cunt, syllable, and you're over. Sit down."

I pushed Hawthorne into a chair. He landed hard.

"I don't really see anything else to secure you with, so I'm gonna have to knock you out with this hammer."

I held the tool aloft, and then I paused and smelled my hand—"Is that your cologne—that's fucking nasty, the ladies like that shit?"

He remained silent, but his eyes darted with purpose toward a rope coiled in the corner of the room.

"Are you trying to tell me something? You really are quite the bitch, you know. I mean, if it was me, and I was torturing someone's loved one, and then I turned around and came face to face with the one who loves—with a fucking hammer in his hand…well, let's just say—I wouldn't'a sat down on the ground and waited until he decided to beat my fucking brains in."

A female voice called from downstairs.

"Hey, they don't carry charcoal lighter, but I got a bottle of 151—it's flammable—we'll toast and roast that fucker!"

I shook my head in disgust at Hawthorne as I held a finger to my lips. I moved across the room to the top of the stairs, but remained out of view—the hammer cocked and ready. I listened as the footsteps ascended—a light, playful teen bounce. As she reached the top of the stairs, I stepped into view and brought the hammer down squarely upon her face—one perfectly placed blow. The mouthy little barista fell backwards—her body tumbled lifeless down the stairs.

"Oh, my, I don't think she's moving."

I walked over to my captive and placed the tip of the hammer's head against my lips. I stuck out my tongue and licked the metal—"Hmmm, non-stick, clean as a whistle. That's a fine little hammer we've got here, John."

Hawthorne closed his eyes—shivering, waiting for the eminent blow. I lightly tapped him on the head with the tool.

"Now, what were you trying to tell me before we were so rudely interrupted?"

As I spoke, Burroughs staggered out of the bedroom and steadied himself against the wall—"Arthur, I want to go."

I moved to my friend and put my hand on his shoulder. The old man looked pale, but still stalwart.

"I got you, Boss—let me load up"—I snatched a chair from the table. The old man sat down as I returned to my captive.

"Where are the keys to Tom's car? Does she got 'em?"—I nodded toward the stairs—"You can speak now."

"They're here in my pocket. I was only…"

"—No, no, that's enough. We're gonna talk later."

I had Hawthorne stand and I took the keys. I steered him toward the stairs—"Be careful here, these are quite steep—we wouldn't want another accident."

Jenny's body lay at the bottom of the landing; her neck was bent in an unnatural angle. She wasn't breathing. Hawthorne and I stepped over her fresh remains.

"Wait a minute, John. I saw how tender you were earlier—I wouldn't want you to part without a sweet kiss."

I pushed Hawthorne toward the body and forced the man to his knees. He bent over and put his lips against her arm.

"Oh no, that won't do. You didn't kiss her arm earlier. As I remember, you rubbed her ass and kissed her right on the lips."

I grabbed the girl's hair and cranked her broken neck towards Hawthorne—her bloody face and wide-open, lifeless eyes inches from the man—"Come on, Johnny, give her a big loving—"

"—Arthur!" Burroughs called.

"I'm coming, Boss. Just saying our good-byes."

I dragged Hawthorne to his feet—tears rolling down his face. I opened the trunk of Burroughs' rental, forced him inside, and slammed the lid. The girl's body I drug off the landing and onto the floor. I climbed the stairs and found Burroughs on his feet—waiting.

"Here, hang on to me."

We made our way slowly down the stairs. When we reached the landing, the old man saw the twisted body of the girl.

"What happened?"

"She fell."

"Hawthorne?"

"He's in the car."

I helped Burroughs into the rental, and I rolled up the steel door. We left without locking up.

"Hang on a minute, Pops. I've gotta make a call."

We drove to the corner and parked near the payphone. It was covered in graffiti, but surprisingly still in working order. I picked up the receiver and dialed "0."

"Hello, this is the operator."

"I need to reach the police, but I don't have any coins. Can you connect me? I need the Harbor Station."

"Is this an emergency?"

"Yeah, but not to me. There's been an accident."

"One moment, please."

As I waited for the connection, I read the graffiti. It seems that if I returned at midnight, I could get a free blowjob. I made a mental note of it.

"1832—this is Officer Walters. What's your emergency?"

"I'd like to speak to Lemke, please."

"Detective Lemke?"

"Yeah, you guys can call him what you want, but…yes, that one, please."

"Hold."

As I waited, I listened to the soft tones of elevator music— cannibalized show tunes that were meant to calm and distract. I laughed, thinking of the police elevators that I'd ridden in—the experience was never pleasant or calming.

"Hello, this is Detective Lemke."

"Lemke, it's Arthur."

"Chance?"

"Yes."

"You're in a lot of trouble, son."

"I figured that—how's Roberts?"

"Where are you? Let me come see you."

"Nah—not tonight. I've got a body for you—a casualty of war, so to speak."

"Tom Burroughs?"

"Burroughs? Why the fuck would I have him? Oh, I get it, because he snitched me out, you think I did him? You fucking pricks are all the same—no honor in thieves, no honor in those that catch 'em, huh?"

"Arthur, where are you?"

"I'm on the corner of Jefferson and Noel—a warehouse apartment—across from what looks to be a pretty good little dim sum place. I left the door open. Send your boys—and the coroner, but be quick."

I hung up the phone.

CHAPTER TWENTY ONE—WHERE'S HANK?

"Arthur, is that the van?"

"Yeah, but we'll get it later."

"Let's get it now. I'll drive it. I don't know what your problem is with that vehicle."

I pulled on to Noel and put the pedal down.

"We're gonna have to come back. I called Lemke."

"What? What'd you call him for?"

"I gave him the dead girl and the warehouse. Hopefully, he rolls up when the cleaners are there. Ha! I'd like to see that."—*Fuck. I'm glad I reached Burroughs in time—he saved me, I saved him. His death would've crushed me. There's plenty of Arthurs in this world—shit, we got two too many right now, but there's only one Burroughs.*—"Fuckin'a Pops, they could've been cleaning you."

"I know"—the old man leaned back in his seat—"I'm too old for this shit."

"You doing okay?"

"I'm alright—let's get back to Gracie's and I'll get straightened out. It's not the first time that I've been slapped around."

"Fuck—I wouldn't wanna fight you—you take a beating like that and you're still willing to drive that van."

He laughed as his eyes took in the city streets.

"Arthur, you missed the highway."

"Nah, we gotta go get Gracie, and if you don't mind, I'd like to pick up a little something"—Burroughs threw me a sideways glance—"Don't worry. I'm not gonna drink and drive."

We stopped at a liquor mart—the large fluorescent sign screamed: $2.99 a bottle.

The good thing about booze is no matter where they sell it, it's always good—you got your quality control—not like some junkie buying a bag of who knows what. You always know what you're getting when you're buying sauce.

I picked up a pint of Popov, some orange juice, and a small package of Wet Wipes. As I walked past the trunk of the car, I slapped it with my hand—"Stay with me, bud. We're almost home."

I passed my purchases to Burroughs as I climbed behind the wheel—"Good"—he went through the bag—"I see you've bought mixer—you're behaving yourself."

"Really? Wow—if you think I'm sticking that fruity shit in my vodka, they hit you harder than I thought. The juice and the wipes are for you—you're still looking a bit pale—shaky, and you could do with a freshening."

"I'm shaky? Have you seen your hands?"

I held out my arm—my fingers trembling—the quick nip of Cutty did nothing for my nerves; I shook my hand and put it back on the wheel—"Do you feel like talking?"

"I'm feeling better—that young woman clanged my bell for sure, but I'm okay"—he wiped the dried blood from his face and took a drink of juice. "When I left this morning, I figured I would start with Abigail, so I went straight to County General—"

"County? You'd think she'd be at Memorial."

"Arthur, why don't you just drive? I'm not feeling well enough to be interrupted"—I conceded by physically zipping my lips—"As I was saying, I went to County General—Abigail's father is a major donor to that institution, so she practically has a wing to herself. As expected, there were security guards everywhere. They weren't going to allow me in, but I caught a break and ran into Guy Hodges—Allston Dupree's personal secretary. I asked him of her welfare—played the part of a concerned family friend—which I am, and he allowed me visitation; but he also accompanied me to her room. He was quite inquisitive—wondered if I'd been up to anything exciting. It seemed a bit strange, under the circumstances—what with Abigail in the hospital and all, but on the other hand, his interest is not uncommon; I often get questions about my comings and goings—you're not the only one with a reputation"—*the old man still had his pride*—"I did find his momentary disappointment at my admission to being retired a bit odd though, but he followed it up with a quick smile"—Burroughs touched at his face with a Wet Wipe—he was looking better, only slightly worse for the wear—"There was security at the elevator doors, as well as her room. Her father's well dressed, licensed, goons were all business—frisked me, for God's sake. When I saw Abigail, she was sitting up, but staring blankly ahead; an untouched tray of food was by her bedside. Her hair had been shorn, but other than that—and a small cut on her lip, there were no visible signs of abuse. I greeted her, but she made no response; she held the same stunned countenance. It was a sad thing."

I remained silent but raised my hand. Burroughs laughed.

"Yes?"

"She's in on it."

"What?"

"Yeah, I overheard a phone call with Hawthorne and my brother. He spoke of her involvement."

"Arthur, that girl was practically comatose—in a fugue, like an animal caught in headlights. She was not, in on it."

"And you, my friend, are becoming gullible in your waning years. According to that Frank, she bailed on Hawthorne—thought he was incompetent, and now she's laying up, waiting for him to self-destruct or, as I'm about to put it to him, get deconstructed."

"But that doesn't make sense, Arthur; what is she getting out of this?"

"Who the fuck knows? What are any of 'em getting—it's drugs, it's not drugs, it's extortion, and then it's not. I've gone through Terry and Paul, and now I'm about to roll through this piece of shit in the trunk, but nobody seems to know what the fuck is going on."

"Yes, and then there's this"—Burroughs fished the locker key from his pocket.

"Ha! Are you shitting me—you had it on you?"

"They didn't even frisk me—unbelievable, considering that this was Hawthorne's object of interest."

"Why would Abigail give me the key if she was working with Hawthorne? It doesn't make any fucking sense."

"Arthur, I have no idea, but when I was a young reporter, I realized that in some situations 'A" correlated directly to 'B' meaning that some cases were clear cut; an accountant goes missing, his body is found, you investigate those for whom he worked, and you turn up a crooked business man who commits murder, or hires someone to commit murder, out of fear of losing his lifestyle. It's elementary, as Holmes might say. But then you have those cases where there is no set path to any one specific goal. It's almost a kaleidoscope of self-centered evil; each part of the whole working with, and yet against, the other players—various sub-schemes within the framework, with no single destination—rather a multitude of goals being pursued beneath the umbrella of an objective—and maybe this is what we've stumbled upon."

"Sounds like a lot of ass-kicking to me."

"Yes, but whose ass?"

I turned on the radio, and to appease the old man, lowered the volume—"Do you think Matsudo's pissed?"

"Arthur, that old boy seems pretty resilient to me—and very fond of you. I'm familiar with his successful attempts to retain his property rights. He's known in some circles as, 'the thorn in Dupree's ass.' I wouldn't worry about him."

"Maybe it's him they want—he's the true target, and I am his Charlie Chan."

"No, you're his drunken, inappropriate tenant"—Burroughs rolled down the window and took a deep breath of early evening air—"By the way, Frank seemed fine."

"I was gonna ask, but you got all pontificating, and I thought I'd give you your stage."

"And that's another thing, pull over."

"Why?"

"Because your house might still be watched. When I arrived earlier today, a black sedan was hovering near the corner."

"Real sleek, late model?"

"Yeah, it could have been your man, but I'm not sure. I saw the car pull away as I parked. They might still be around."

"But I wanna see Frank."

"I'm sure you do, but not yet"—the old man surveyed the neighborhood—"There; you can mark time at the bus station. I'm sure you can find some interesting diversions as you wait."

I pulled to the curb, and Burroughs took the wheel.

"Are you sure you're okay to drive?"

"Yes. I'm fine."

"Hand me my bottle."

"No."

"God damn it."

Burroughs put the car in gear.

"Hey, don't forget you got 'fuck nut' in the trunk. I don't want you doing donuts in the street—getting arrested and having to explain him."

The bus station was filthy—stained plastic benches and a sidewalk grey linoleum floor. There were a few travelers, but most of them seemed as if they were going nowhere; for them, the bus station was the destination, a refuge from the cold.

I sat below a TV set with a screen covered with loogies. I could barely make out the picture through the haze of dried spit. They were broadcasting an old movie—one I'd seen many times. The sound was unintelligible, but I knew the words...

"What a pity, her manners don't match her looks..."

I've always loved that line. Quite apropos for the two fucks that I just dispatched—well, one dead, and one on the way.

The innards of the Greyhound station felt like a county ward and I soon tired of the florescent light depression. I wandered outside and bummed a smoke off a street urchin. At the liquor mart across the street, I picked up a pack of matches and a pocket size bottle of vodka—a short freeway flyer.

It sure felt good going down, but the economy taste of alcohol touched that space in me that said, just-one-more, and instead of bringing comfort, it brought desire.

I went back for another. By the time Burroughs and Gracie arrived, I was six or seven short dogs deep.

I stumbled up to the car—"Let me drive."

Burroughs locked the door. "Sit in the back or walk."

"Come on, fucker."

Gracie had a look of disgust on her face as I walked by her window. I sat in the back.

"You see, Gracie, the great misconception of many drunks is that vodka can't be smelled on one's breath, and yet, the sot in the backseat disproves that notion."

"Alright, laugh it up, asshole. Gracie, will you please remind that old man that he should be dead"—I stretched out across the seat—"and besides, it's fucking cold outside—I needed a warm-up."

The ride back to Gracie's was uneventful and sobering.

"Tom"—Gracie pointed to a side drive—"if you pull behind the building, there's a bungalow in the back. I was going to convert it, but I haven't got around to it yet—we use it for storage."

The old man drove behind the motel. There was an outer building in a wooded area—hidden from the street.

"Back the car in and give me the keys, I'll get Hank to unload"—she looked back at me—"Coffee?"

"No. I've got a little something in the bag"—she stared me down—"Yeah, on second thought, I think I will have a cup of black and maybe a piece of bread or something. I'm starving."

We followed Gracie up front; on the walkway, we ran into Hank.

"Hey, buddy"—Gracie handed him the keys—"Arthur has a package in the trunk of the car. Could you please get it out and secure it in the bungalow?"

"Sure thing, Gracie"—he began to walk away, but then paused—"Is it fragile?"

"It's not fragile, but don't break it, okay?"

We got cleaned up and walked over to the chicken place. I got the Big Rooster combo and Burroughs, the Henny Penny box. Gracie abstained.

"I'd tell you to lay off the meat," she said, "but I think that vodka is made from pig testicles, and you'll never let that go."

I spit root beer through my nose—"God damn it! This was a fresh shirt."

"Believe me, polyester boy, that root beer stain is an improvement."

"Surprisingly, the chicken wasn't bad, Gracie"—Burroughs wiped grease from his chin—"but I'll give you the full report after my...uh...morning constitutional."

"Hey, Pops, are you in on this?" I gestured toward the bungalow.

He shook me off.

"I'm tired, Arthur; I think I'll sit this out, but there is one thing I'd like to talk about"—he turned to Gracie—"It seems as if your involvement in our situation has deepened. Are you okay with that?"

"I'm okay, Tom. There are a few things I need to get my head around—and I think you and I have a long talk on the horizon, but for now, don't worry about me. I'm my mother's daughter—only more so."

She kissed him on the forehead.

Burroughs turned to me—"You be cool, okay?"

"I've got Gracie looking out for me—what could go wrong?"

Burroughs went to his room as Gracie and I walked towards the back.

"I met Frank."

"What?"

"Your cat, Frank."

"Oh, fuck, man, I thought you meant my—how was he?"

Gracie stopped on the blacktop.

I could see Hank standing behind the front desk—he seemed pleased as my eyes met his.

"Frank was adorable, and I like the old man—he's a cool customer"—she straightened a loose paver with her foot—"After we talk to your uh…friend, you and I are gonna get on the same page."

"A sleepover?"

"No. The last time I had a man in my bed with alcohol on his breath was almost two years ago, and I'll make no exception for you."

The hotel and the bungalow had been in Gracie's family for generations—the buildings, and a few undeveloped acres were all that remained of her family's homestead. I liked the feel of the place. It was secluded within the city. I could see why Gracie wanted to refurbish it.

We stepped onto the wide porch, and Gracie opened the door. There was a bare light bulb hanging from a black cord in the ceiling and the shades on the windows were down. Hawthorne had been beaten—he was naked, gagged, blindfolded, and tied to a chair in the center of the room—shivering. The light hung directly over his head.

"Fucking Hank."

"He *was* smiling as we walked by."

"Of course, he was"—Gracie undid the gag in Hawthorne's mouth—"he's a fucking child. Goddamn it."

A knock fell twice upon the bungalow door. It opened and Hank popped his head in.

"Excuse me, are we renting number five or is the heat still out?"

"Are you fucking kidding me? Look at this!"

He beamed with pride—"You said he wasn't fragile—and he resisted."

"You're a fucking idiot—get out of here—and don't rent five!"

She turned her attention to Hawthorne, pulled off his blindfold, and gave him a hard slap to the face. It shook him up.

"Arthur, get that fucking blanket and put it around him."

I did as I was asked—our captive seemed grateful.

Gracie spoke quiet in my ear, "He probably raped him—Hank can be a bit barbaric at times, but he's good at the desk"—she stepped back and pulled up a chair—"Go to work, Baby."

Hawthorne stared in terror.

"I'm sorry about Hank, John, especially if he…uh…violated you—and if that's the case, I'm sure Gracie will have a word with him. First off, since we've had no proper introduction, I'd like to introduce myself, I'm Arthur Chance. It's a pleasure to meet you"— I stuck out my hand and pretended to shake—"Good, now that we've dispensed with the pleasantries, I'd like to get down to business."

Hawthorne tightened his body and braced for the blow.

"Oh no. I'm not gonna lay a hand on you—and neither will Gracie nor Hank—as long as you answer honestly and are forthcoming—give me more than I ask—you'll walk out of this room unscathed. I can't speak for Burroughs though—I'm sure he'd love to give you a good thrashing, but I think he went to bed—isn't that right, Gracie?"

"That's correct, Arthur."

"See, John, we're getting it done civilized—unlike how you and your late girlfriend treated my partner. I hope she wasn't too precious"—I took off my jacket—"Gracie, I hope you got a good memory, because I'm expecting Mr. Hawthorne to open up with all sorts of information, and I've got no pen or paper to jot it down."

"I've got it, Arthur."

"Are you sure?"

"I've got it."

"Excellent"—I leaned toward my captive—practically nose to nose—"Okay—how the fuck am I involved with this?"

"Your brother—I was approached by him—we met through mutual friends. He said he had a problem that I could help him with—a reporter, Grayson, was investigating him. Your brother said he had a way out of it, and he brought me in."

"You're doing quite well, John. If you continue like this, things will go as I said. You'd like that, correct?"

"Yes."

"Would you like to walk out of here?"

"Yes."

"Well, I assure you, I'm a man of my word"—I casually paced as a lawyer before the bench—"And did Frank tell you what that way was?"

"Yes."

"Speak up."

"He said he had a brother—in his words; a loser who lived near the harbor. He said that you and he are identical twins, and that he was going to pin things on you, and then…"

"Yes."

"He said he was going to have you killed."

"I object!" I turned to Gracie. "Could you imagine, I took a fucking beating for that little prick when we were kids, and after all these years, he tries this with me?"

I spoke to Hawthorne, "You see, John. That was big news—upsetting news to most people—terrifying even, and I didn't lay a hand on you; I'm not even angry. You should feel good about that—continue."

"The girl, Nikki, she took your keys, and we broke into your place—I have your knife."

"On you?"—I looked to Gracie—"Did the big dummy just beat him or did he happen to go through his pockets as he was fucking him?"

"Arthur."

"It's at the warehouse, in a plastic bag—Nikki's blood is…" Hawthorne hesitated.

"Is?"

"It's on the knife—I didn't kill her, your brother did. He used your knife when he offed the girl. Her blood is all over it."

I spoke to Gracie. "Now, that knife thing is gonna be an issue, I was fucking around and sent the cops to the warehouse"—I turned back to John—"Would it have been easy to find? I mean—it didn't look like you tidied up much."

"It was on the counter—in plain sight."

"Motherfucker!"

Hawthorne cowered—*I took a deep breath and gave a slow, deliberate, count-to-six exhale*—"Okay, it'll be alright. I love that fucking knife—it's badass Gracie—I've had it for years."

"Arthur."

"Sorry"—I smoothed my collar—"John, please continue—He's doing quite well, isn't he Gracie?"

"Quite well, Arthur. This is beyond enlightening—I love

your part in it."

"Humph—go on."

"I was supposed to drop the knife when I dumped Nikki's body, but I forgot."

"You forgot or you fucked up?"

"I fucked up—I went back to do it, but they were already on her."

"The cops?"

"Yeah—crazy quick—too fast, like they were tipped."

"Tipped?"

"Like they saw me dump her—who knows?"

"And why the photos, Nikki, and then Abigail?"—*Shit, I fucked both of 'em. We don't need that...uh*...I turned to Gracie— "You know, we gotta lot of ground to cover here, in case you got something else to do."

"I'm fine, Arthur"—she smiled—"I've got all night."

"The photos were your brother's idea. He said you had a drinking problem—a black-out drunk he called you. I think he was toying with you—trying to get you to kill yourself—he said it ran in the family."

"That's what he thinks"—I looked to Gracie—"You know, he was right about that though—I almost did it—Burroughs stopped me. I was ready to roll."

"The night you stayed here?"

"The next day, yeah, I left here to do it."

Gracie glared at Hawthorne.

"The photos weren't just for you, Arthur. I was to send an envelope to the police."

"Did you?"

"No, They're still…"

"In the warehouse with the knife?" Gracie asked.

"Yes."

"Did you bother looking around while you were in there? You jumped all over Hank, thinking he hadn't been thorough, and you basically rolled in blind—I guess, 'you spot it, you got it'—right Champ?"

"Fuck off, Gracie. I found the hammer—that place was a fucking mess. He doesn't keep a clean house, and I wasn't on a fucking scavenger hunt"—I pressed Hawthorne—"Was there anything else left in that shithole that I should know about? Think hard. I don't wanna be upset later."

Hawthorne closed his eyes.

I could almost see him stumbling across his memories.

"The drug—there's a vial of Hypno in my jacket."

I stood quietly for a moment—"Is that what Nikki gave me on the pier?"

"Yes."

"Is this what you gave Abigail?"—*Hawthorne hesitated. I could read his distress*—"Don't hold back, John. Think about it. Do you really want to get hurt for a lie?"

"No."

"No, what?"

"She never took it."

"Bullshit. She showed me photos of her on it."

"She showed you photos of her getting fucked. She never took anything."

"Why?"

"Because she's fucked up—that bitch is out of her mind."

I smiled at Gracie—"It seems they're having a bit of a lovers' spat—she bailed on him." I walked over and touched Gracie's hair—"You know, this checks out with what Paul said—she might not have been drugged."

Gracie playfully pulled away—"Was that before or after you kicked him in the stomach?"

"The photos were her idea," Hawthorne continued, "She wanted to shoot naughty pictures. They weren't part of the deal. Fuck, I was shocked when I saw them at your place—you imagine that, the woman you love sharing those with another man. She was the one who brought in Dick Heavy."

"And how would she know him?"

"Oh, like rich little girls don't like porn—wake up. Why don't you talk to her about her sexual issues—you fucked her."

I raised my hand to Hawthorne—a punch to follow, but then I pulled it back.

"You're getting a real attitude, Johnny—pushing my restraint"—I stepped away and looked around the room—searching for a diversion—"I've broken my word before, and I'm sure if I go against my promise and flay the skin off your face, I'm not gonna beat myself up over it."

"She was never supposed to speak to you—or give you that key. She was doing whatever the fuck she felt like—thinks she's above and smarter than everyone—and now I'm here and she doesn't give a fuck."

"It seems like he's hurt that you fucked his girlfriend, Stud," Gracie laughed as she spoke.

"Hey, fuck you, Gracie. It was only two times—two fucking times, and to be honest, it wasn't that good"—I tuned back to Hawthorne—"You know, rich girls are shitty in bed—I mean, she was better than most, but…"

"Arthur."

"Yeah"—I frowned at Hawthorne—"So why did she come to me?"

"Because she's crazy. She's playing with you—told me that she was going to use you to find that locker—she gets off on it—walking the edge she called it, but then she runs back to her daddy and leaves me hanging. It was supposed to be a simple deal—pin Nikki's murder on you and plant the knife. I shouldn't even fucking be here."

Hawthorne began to cry, and once rolling, he couldn't stop.

We walked outside and let him bawl.

Gracie kissed me on the porch.

"Ughhh, that's fucking nasty"—she wiped the taste of

alcohol off her lips—"I hate vodka."

"That's ridiculous—you can't even smell it—and who the fuck hates vodka? What are you, a whiskey girl?"

"I'm a sober girl."

I leaned against the porch railing—looked up to a crescent moon—"Do you think he has anymore in him?"

"Tonight? I don't think so—unless you press him physically. I do enjoy watching you work. You're quite good at it— unorthodox—borderline psychotic, but very effective."

"I do my best"—I put my arms around her and kissed the back of her neck. She pushed me away.

"I think we're done for the night, Stud, but we can't leave him like that."

"Tied up?"

"Naked."

We walked back inside. Hawthorne was still lightly sobbing. I untied him—"Put your clothes on."

Hawthorne dressed as Gracie and I stood by.

"Where are his shoes?" I looked around the floor.

"Hank probably has them."

"Why'd he take his fucking shoes? Forget it—don't tell me—You know, I once knew a kid who collected men's pants— used, dirty trousers; he kept 'em neatly folded beneath his bed. I'm not sure what he did with 'em but…"—as I told my tale, Gracie, with professional knots, resecured Hawthorne to the chair and wrapped the blanket around him.

"Does he need the gag?"

"No. If he screams, the only one who'll hear him is Hank, and I don't think our boy here wants that shoe stealing Romeo to come check him out."

Gracie turned out the light.

CHAPTER TWENTY-TWO—SADDLE UP

I sat at the table. My mother sat two seats to my right. Burroughs stood in the front of the room, holding a tray laden with food—"It's not all yours, Arthur."

The old man placed the tray on the table and crossed the floor to a pair of doublewide doors. A bright golden light swept in waves through the keyhole. Burroughs passed his hand through the beam and the doors opened. My grandmother walked into the room, followed by a procession of monks—each friar carrying a deceased duplicate of Frank in his arms. My mother put her hands over her face as the room filled beyond capacity. She bent over her plate and her tears and dark brunette curls pooled on the table.

"I'm sorry, Mother. I should've known better."

Burroughs appeared behind me and placed his hand on my shoulder.

"You shouldn't have known at all," he said.

The morning light staggered through the blinds and fell across my face. I climbed out of bed and took a swig from a large coffee that was orphaned on the table—it was lukewarm, but it was black—semi-satisfying. Burroughs' bed had been made and the room somewhat straightened.

"Fuck. I must have been out of it."

I was slightly groggy, but my body felt strong—better than I had felt in weeks. I got dressed and walked outside. Burroughs was in a chair by the door—smoking the tired end of yesterday's cigar. I sat beside him.

"Good morning, Princess," said the old man, "looks like you got your beauty sleep."

"Yeah, fuck. What time is it?"

"A bit past ten."

"In the morning?"

Burroughs looked up to a clear blue sky and shielded his eyes from the sun—"Yeah, pretty much."

"Can I get the shorts on that?"

He handed me the cigar—"Have at it, my friend—mind the blood."

I looked at Burroughs' face and saw a slight cut on his upper lip—a bruise on his cheek—"Fucking bitch, man, she should've got a real beating…"

Burroughs silenced me—"I think your retribution was more than enough."

"Yeah, but she didn't see it coming—speaking of that…"

Gracie walked up.

She was dressed in a pair of thin black boots, tight straight leg pants to match, and a black t-shirt—her hair was pulled off her face and tied behind."

"Well, don't you look 'all business,'" I said, "How's our boy?"

"I had to chase Hank away from his room, but other than that, I think he's ready to continue."

"Is he all right?"

"He was cold and tired of the chair, but yeah—he's still breathing."

"I meant Hank—that fucking dude is out-there, man. What are you doing with him?"

"Arthur, I'd trust Hank with my life—and have many times. He's a good right hand…"

"Yeah, a right hand down his pants—it's fucking creepy."

Gracie leaned against a post near the door; she bent down and pulled a silver nail file from her boot.

"Hank has a funny theory. He's gentle as a lamb to the innocents—wouldn't raise a hand against a child or an average citizen, but when it comes to people like Hawthorne—and others of his ilk, Hank considers them 'free game.' He once told me that they made the decision to enter into the world of the animal, so that's what he gives them—an animal. I find it fascinating. You should get to know him."

"Not today—I've got enough on my plate, besides, I'd like to keep my boots on."

"It sounds like I missed something," said Burroughs.

"Believe me," I replied, "your old ass didn't need to see any of that noise."

I got my end lit and took a puff.

"I'd like to step inside and plan our day," said Burroughs. "Gracie filled me in, but even so, I think I still have more questions than answers."

We pulled up around the small table in our room; Gracie and Burroughs in the chairs—I sat on the corner of the bed.

"The Abigail issue saddens me," said Burroughs. "I've watched her since she was a small child"—he shook his head—"and coming from privilege."

"Yeah, well, fuck privilege—a bunch of entitled shits, if you ask me. I've never met a rich man who, in getting all he wants, doesn't want more."

Gracie laughed—"Arthur, the philosopher. Will you be breaking out the brass knuckles today, Plato?"

"Fuck you, Gracie."

"What are we to do with our, uh…visitor?" said Burroughs.

"I've been thinking…"

Gracie and the old man groaned.

"Fuck both of you! I know what's up—and remember, we're still in a situation, Tom. Abigail is holed up in that hospital, and we can't get a hand on her. Terry was worthless…"

"And he's got a fucked-up car."

I gave Gracie the evil eye—"Heavy and Paul were only in it for the money and Nikki is dead."

"And Jenny," said Burroughs.

"Yeah, and Jenny, but I only did one of 'em."

"Speaking of that, Arthur," said Burroughs, "where's the hammer?"

"It's uh…still at the warehouse."

"Yes, with the knife, your fingerprints and Nikki's blood. Are you forgetting the police? They basically have you dead to rights on two homicides."

"They don't got shit."

"What?"

"Yeah, Lemke said they had no prints on me—which I find fucking ridiculous, but he wanted to catch a set of 'em before they found Abi's car. I split before he rolled me."

"But you have old cases—they were sure to have something."

"That's what I said, but nope, nothing."

"Prints don't just disappear, Arthur."

"Yeah, no shit, Gracie, and fucking mystery twin brothers don't reappear out of thin air either, right? This whole fucking thing is whacked."

Burroughs stood and walked to the window—"What if those prints weren't randomly lost? What if Frank had something to do with it?"

"What if, what if, I'm fucking sick of "what if"…and that brings me to my objective—I say it's time to visit my brother—give him a little taste of what's up—we can use Hawthorne to lead us there."

Gracie casually filed her nails—"And what if Hawthorne doesn't know where he is?"

"—And," Burroughs said, "what do you think your brother is going to do when we get there—admit his mistakes, turn himself in, take full responsibility for his crimes, and reconcile with you?"

"I'm not a fucking fortune teller, man, but if you two are being straight, you'll recognize that we got nothing else. That piece of shit in the bungalow can't stay there forever. I say we use him, and get this shit wrapped up—I miss Frank, man. I wanna go home"

I was too long in the outside world. I want my little man. I want the door closed behind my back, a view of the harbor through glass, I want a book and a couch—soft pajamas, and a warm muted trumpet playing comfort on my hi-fi. I want my home.

I lay back on the bed.

Gracie put her hand on my knee—"I can't believe I'm gonna say this but, Arthur's right. As far as I can see, we've got nothing. They—whoever they are, are gonna realize that Hawthorne is missing, if they haven't done so already, and when they do, that door is gonna close. I'm not a fan of jumping in without caution, but sometimes you've gotta move quick and aggressively."

"Exactly"—I sat up and smoothed my hair—"That's it, Baby, just like she said. I'm right, let's roll!"

Gracie shook her head—"That right there is a touch unnerving, but I do think it's time to press Hawthorne and move ahead."

When Burroughs walked into the room, Hawthorne's eyes lit with terror. My promise of non-violence didn't extend to the old man, and Hawthorne knew that he had one coming. Burroughs took a seat in the corner. I approached.

"Good morning, John. Do you remember our deal from yesterday—I don't hurt you, if you keep talking? Did you say hello to Tom?"

Hawthorne agreed as he acknowledged Burroughs with his eyes.

"Excellent. Now, I'd like to refresh a few things"—I pulled up a chair and sat face to face with my captive—"Dick Heavy and the midget, Paul, their involvement was only on the photo end of things?"

"Yes."

"Were they there when my brother killed Nikki?"

"No. They set me up with the gear—Frank didn't want them around. The girl thought we were doing a straight shoot, and then your brother drugged and killed her."

"With my knife?"

"Yes."

"Who was she to him?"

"No one. I don't think Frank cares much for women."

I turned to Burroughs—"This all checks out. John is being a very good boy"—I smiled at Hawthorne—"You didn't think you were the only one we were talking to, did you?"

"No. I didn't."

"Good for you, John, and another excellent reason for you to play it straight—if we get a conflicting story, I'm turning on the heat."

"I'm telling you right. I've got no reason to lie."

"—About Abigail and your porn business?"

"Her porn business. It was her idea to shoot society girls. She hates them. She thought it was funny."

"Jesus, you are the rat, aren't you?"

"A real little bitch," said Gracie. I frowned at her.

"And how did you meet dear Abigail?"

"Your brother. Abigail approached me at a party. She came up sly—asked me how the Grayson thing was going, and then she laughed and walked away."

"Was she sleeping with Frank?"

"I don't know, yeah, probably, he was pretty familiar with his touch—she liked having him around."

"And she lured you into a life of crime. That's a sad tale."

"No"—for a moment, Hawthorne closed his eyes.

"That's okay, John. We'll be paying her a visit soon."

I turned to Burroughs. "You good, Boss?"

"Just about"—Burroughs looked to Hawthorne. "Do you know who killed Grayson?"

"Frank did it. He laughed about how he fell—said he floated like a leaf until he hit the bay."

"And what's in the locker?"

"I don't know, but Frank was worried—he's not the end of the line here."

"What do you mean?"

"I mean he answers to someone."

"Do you know who that is?"

Hawthorne hesitated momentarily before he spoke—"No."

Gracie shook her head at me—she wasn't buying.

"John?"

"I don't know. I'm being straight, man. Please, Arthur. I'm telling you the truth."

"Personally, I don't give a fuck whose dick my brother is sucking. This clown is dry. Let's wrap this up"—I kicked my chair out of the way—"Do you know where Frank is?"

"Yes, he's in the Heights."

"Is he well protected?"

"There's a guard gate, but it's a single property."

"What about goons? Anything?"

"A house-keeper, but she's an old woman."

"Do you know the lay of his place—would it be strange if you went there?"

"Yeah, I know it—I do things for him. I'm in and out."

"Is he armed?"

"Fuck, I don't know. I've seen him with a piece, and he talks big, but he's not strapped, if you know what I mean."

"Do you got a car?"

"Yes."

"Where is it?"

"Parked across from the warehouse."

"The keys?"

"On the counter next to the knife."

"Motherfucker!" I kicked Hawthorne's chair—"I fucking told you—if there was anything in there that I needed to know about, that you'd better spill it!"

"Fuck, don't kill me. I didn't know. My keys—why would that matter?"

Gracie put a calming hand on my back. I took a deep breath—"I apologize, John—and you're right, your keys won't matter"—I turned to Gracie and Burroughs—"Are you two ready-to-roll?"

"I'm good," said Burroughs.

"I've gotta grab a few things," said Gracie, "but yeah, I'm down."

"All right, you get your shit. I'm gonna take fucknut in Burroughs' rental. You two are gonna take the minivan."

"Arthur."

"Yeah, boss?"

"You left the van at the warehouse."

"God damn it."

CHAPTER TWENTY-THREE—BROTHER

I walked back to our room and broke out my .38. I loaded the gun and tucked a few loose rounds into my pocket. The Colt felt comfortable in my hand, and when I tucked it down the front of my slacks, my cock got hard. I pulled my t-shirt over the walnut handgrip, and I brushed my hair to the side. I checked my look in the mirror and blew myself a kiss before I left the room.

Gracie was in conversation with Burroughs—"You don't have to go with us. We don't know what we're getting into."

"I'd rather be there, than pacing the floor here. I don't like worrying about the boy."

I put my hand on his shoulder—"I got this, man."

"What you've got is a hard-on, Champ," Gracie laughed, "from the look of it—a snub nose erection."

I looked down at my pants and puffed out my shirt.

"Your slacks are too tight for that shit. Anyone solid would see it in a second"—she patted my crotch—"Do you have it tucked into your panties?"

"Yeah, but…"—I attempted to draw the gun from my under--pants, but it got caught on my waistband.

"Jesus Christ, you're gonna get yourself killed. Hang tight."

Gracie jogged off toward her room.

"Arthur, are you familiar with that weapon?"

"It's a gun, it's loaded, and I squeeze the trigger. My father had one just like it—I fired that—no problem. Okay, Chief?" I rolled the chamber and replaced the gun in my slacks.

"You're going to shoot your pecker off."

Gracie returned with a leather holster. She held out her hand—"Let's see it, killer."

I handed her the gun.

"This is nice, 1950s Cobra—I thought you were a knife man"—she checked to see if it was loaded, and then she spun it in her hand and gave it butt first to Burroughs—"Where's your jacket, Arthur?"

"In the room."

"Go get it."

I returned with my jacket, and Gracie fit the holster to my frame.

"Do you know how to use that thing?"

"Yes—of course."

"Well, hopefully you won't have to, but better safe than sorry"—she stood back—"try that."

I drew the pistol a few times, and then I replaced it to stay.

We walked back to the bungalow and I steered Hawthorne into the car. Our captive seemed grateful to be riding in a seat.

We stopped around the corner from the warehouse. Gracie retrieved the van, and then climbed back in with the boys and me.

"What's your call, Baby?"

"I figured I'd ride over with, fucknut, here"—I turned to our captive—"Do you ever drive or ride with Frank?"

"Yeah, usually in his car, but sometimes in mine."

"Will the guard hold us up on the way in?"

"Not in my car, no—but he doesn't know this one so, yeah, he probably will."

"But on a quick glance, I'll pass for Frank, right?"

"Yeah—spitting fucking image, but this seems crazy."

"How 'bout you keep your opinion to yourself before you get a smack?"

"I'm going to have to agree, Arthur," said Burroughs, "What if they know he's missing? What if they're ready for this?"

"Look at this guy"—I nodded toward Hawthorne—"he broke like a bitch—no offense, Johnny. He couldn't wait to drop a dime on his partners. I'll bet they know he's got no heart—they won't think he's been snatched; they'll think he ran."

"That's a lot of conjecture," said Gracie.

"Yeah, it is—but I don't got a lot of options—unless you've got something better."

Neither Burroughs nor Gracie spoke.

"That's what I thought."

"If the guard thinks you're Frank, he won't hold us up. Frank calls him a fifteen dollar an hour hard on—he's not a player."

"See," I said, "he knows what's up."

"*He* doesn't want to be tied to a chair," Gracie said.

"And...he also doesn't wanna get shot at the guard gate. Do you, asshole?"

"No, I don't."

"Okay," Gracie said, "so you go in with him and what do we do, follow you in—tell the guard we're there for a pool party? Come on."

"No, of course not. You and Burroughs hang back—I'll bring him out."

"You don't even know what the fucking place looks like—we're gonna just park at the gate and wait?"

"Park down the street."

Hawthorne cut in—"The house is on a curve; they won't see you from the gate."

"Hey, fucker"—Gracie leaned over and grabbed Hawthorne by the shirt—"if any of this is bullshit, I'll personally put one in your fucking head."

"I've got no allegiance to Frank. I want out of this"—Hawthorne turned to me—"When you take him you'll cut me loose, right?"

"You've got my word, man. You get me to Frank, and I'll cut you loose."—I turned to Gracie—"All right?"

"Not all right, but I guess we have nothing else."

Gracie and Burroughs got out of the car. As the old man went to shut his door, I put my hand on his arm.

"Hey, Pops, I don't know how many lives you got left in you, but I'd appreciate you getting the fuck out of there if things go south, okay?"

"Okay, Arthur."

"Fucking liar."

A block away from the house, I pulled over to the curb and took the keys out of the ignition. I told Hawthorne to get behind the wheel. I walked back to the van. Gracie rolled down the window.

"What's up?"

"I feel pretty good about this."

"You came back to tell us that?"

"Yeah, and to thank you. This has been a fucked-up deal, and I know I'm not out of it yet, but I'm feeling better about where I'm at—more in control—if you know what I mean."

"Yeah," said Gracie, "you're a fucking control freak. Can we get this going now?"

"Yeah, Baby! That's the attitude I was looking for."

I slapped the side of the minivan and walked back to the rental. I got in the passenger side and handed Hawthorne the keys.

"So, what are we looking at when we drive in? What's the layout?"

"Frank's office is right off the drive."

"Will he be in there?"

"If he's home—he makes book from there—a wall of closed-circuit TVs—it's there or bed. At this hour he's guaranteed."

"Guaranteed? You're such a cunt. What about anyone else?"

"Maybe the maid, but—"

"—Is she a problem?"

"No, she's a total bitch, but she's usually in the back watching her programs—fucking woman is practically deaf—you can hear the shows blasting in the other room."

"Frank's cool with that?"

"I don't think he gives a fuck."

"Alright, remember what I told you—this fucks up and you're the first to go. Got it?"

"Yes."

"Drive on."

We drove toward the house and pulled into the secluded drive. It was as Hawthorne said—on the bend in the road, not visible from the street. The minivan passed behind us as we pulled up to the gate. Hawthorne rolled down his window and stuck out his head.

The guard approached from the shack—"Does he know you're coming?"—He bent down and looked through the window. His eyes fell on me.

I stepped heavy on him—"Open the fucking gate."

The guard startled and moved back—"I'm sorry, Mr. James. I didn't see you."

He jogged back to his shack and released the wrought iron barrier. We drove through.

"Mr. James? What the fuck is that shit?"

"That's Frank's last name."

"No, it isn't—it's Chance—like his fuck of a father."

The house was beyond ear or gunshot blast from the gate. Hawthorne pulled to the end of the drive and stopped the car. He expected to be freed.

"You're getting out, bud. Lead me in. And if you think you're gonna pull some shit and overpower me, you've got another think coming. Gracie will be on you in a second. I told her, give me a few minutes, then come in blazing."

"I won't—I took you this far, didn't I?"

"Yeah, you're a real prince. Let's go."

We exited the car and walked up a wide stone path to a large ornate door. I stood directly behind Hawthorne as he knocked twice and walked in. Frank was wearing a white suit and sitting on the front of his desk—his feet were bare.

"What the fuck are you doing here?" he said.

"He's dying"—I stepped out from behind Hawthorne and put a bullet through his head. Hawthorne's lifeless body fell to the ground—"What's up, brother?"

Frank stood terrified before me, shaking, and then as if he wasn't witness to the killing, he looked down at Hawthorne's body.

"Oh, you fucking did it now, Arthur; what the fuck were you thinking? We're all dead—you and everybody you fucking love are gone."

"No, 'hello', no, 'nice to see you'? You'd think that after all this time…"

Frank knelt down and touched Hawthorne's body—hoping for a sign of life—"He's Dupree's son, you fucking idiot. Allston is going to kill us."

"Dupree's son?"

"Yes, you fuck—he'll have me killed. He'll have us both killed."

"Does Dupree know that he was fucking his sister?"

Frank glared at me—"This isn't a joke. We're fucking dead."

"Get up"—I pointed the gun at Frank, and he rose to his feet—"I don't give a fuck about that fat prick. You've got a score to settle for me. You're gonna answer for a murder, and I'm going back to my life."

"You aren't going anywhere. This isn't going to get straightened out. Listen to me! They're going to kill us for this. They'll do everyone you've ever loved—I've seen it. Arthur, we're fucking done for—we've gotta go, please…brother, please."

It's a strange thing when you face yourself, and your eyes are those of a coward—a small time hustler running a game to survive—Frank was the worst part of me, personified.

The gypsy woman wondered if I could pull the trigger—do myself in when the time came—would I have the balls to kill the person I hated—and loved most—and now, I knew what she meant. Could I kill myself?

As Gracie walked into the room, I put three slugs into my brother.

CHAPTER TWENTY-FOUR—GOODBYE MR. CHANCE

The scent of gunpowder and the distant sounds of a Mexican soap opera hung in the air. I grinned at Gracie.

"Anyone else?" she said.

"One. Down the hall."

"Give me your gun."

I handed the weapon to Gracie, and she disappeared down the hallway. A moment later, I heard a single shot, and then the TV was silenced.

I looked at my brother's hands—they lay so delicate against the floor. The knuckles weren't scarred—the nails polished and clean.

My mother must have loved this boy—she loved me, and yet, there's no remnant of her love in this room. The ghost of our father stands above me. This is his doing.

Gracie reentered the room. She stood next to me and without a word, returned the gun to my hand.

Burroughs slowly opened the front door and stepped inside. He surveyed the carnage—"Was he armed?"

My voice was without emotion—"Yeah, with a bunch of bullshit threats."

I filled them in on what my brother said about Hawthorne and Dupree.

"Did you believe him?" Burroughs asked.

"He put his life on it, so, yeah—I believe I'm fucked."

"So, what now?" Gracie said.

"I don't know, other than me dying—so what I love can live, I don't see any way out of this."

I thought I'd dodged a bullet, but I guess when you got one coming it's gonna find you sooner or later...my father, my brother, and now me...

"Arthur," said Burroughs, "give me the gun."

Gracie stepped back.

I looked at the Colt, and then I slowly raised my hand. As the gun reached my waist, I smiled at Burroughs. I felt the weight of the piece and closed my eyes.

"Arthur, come on now—give me the gun."

I took a deep breath...

Come on Arthur, just do it...you're better than your father, better than Frank...you're a man of purpose and honor. You had no trouble driving towards that cliff—you were in, man, 100%"...

But maybe that's all I had in me, one selfless moment in a selfish life and now I don't wanna do it...

Come on, dude, just fucking pull it, don't be a cunt, think about your little man...you're a fucking hard-charger, Baby— you're a fucking killer, come on, do it.

...I can't...I can't do it...I'm a coward...

I lowered my head and shamefully handed Burroughs the gun.

The old man walked to the desk and picked up Frank's phone. He dialed a local number.

"Officer Lemke, please."

"Detective," I said.

A moment passed. The sound of elevator music trickled through the receiver. The old man's hand was shaking.

"Charles, it's Tom Burroughs. I killed Arthur Chance. Could you please send someone? I'm at 203 Hartford—in the Heights"— a momentary silence and then—"Yes, I'm alright, but please hurry."

The old man hung up the phone.

"What the fuck are you doing?"

Burroughs pointed at Frank with the gun—"If it's as you said, Arthur…this is the only way. I'll tell them that he is you—they don't have your prints."

"Yeah, that's not gonna work, man. He's clean—the scar, they'll know it's not me."

Burroughs stood over the body and squeezed the trigger— the bullet tore its way through the skull over Frank's left eye.

"They won't now. Gracie, get Arthur the fuck out of here."

As Gracie and I walked to the van, we passed an empty guard shack.

In the evening edition, the headline story carried the news that a respected newsman had killed a local investigator who was wanted for murder. They listed a count of the four confirmed dead, and they acknowledged that no charges were to be filed against Tom Burroughs, long time resident of Ocean Park.

Prologue

A 1948 Italian Crème Cadillac convertible pulled into the parking lot of the Port Authority terminal. A tall blonde man stepped from the car. He wore dark wraparound sunglasses and an exquisitely tailored beige suit—courtesy of Roscoe's. He was 38 years old and attractive—in a dangerous "devil may care" way. He entered the building and approached the information counter. The counter girl's eyes brightened as he smiled.

"Good afternoon, Miss. You look quite lovely today"—she lightly touched her hair—"I was wondering if you could help me. My brother is a real clown—an asshole—alcoholic if you will. He loves to play practical jokes—that is, when he's not drunk or lazing about—anyway, he stole my watch—an expensive gift from our father, and then he told me that he'd placed it here, in a locker, and he gave me this key."

JACK GRISHAM

The Pulse Of The World

JACK GRISHAM WAS BORN IN ALAMEDA COUNTY, CALIFORNIA IN 1961—THE YEAR DASHIELL HAMMETT DIED. THIS FACT IS COMPLETELY UNRELATED TO THE CASE.

ALSO BY JACK GRISHAM

AN AMERICAN DEMON
UNTAMED
CODE BLUE—A LOVE STORY
I WISH THERE WERE MONSTERS
A PRINCIPLE OF RECOVERY

AVAILABLE WORLDWIDE

Made in the USA
Las Vegas, NV
10 December 2022